I0687757

RUNNING SCARED

ROCKSTAR LOVE IS COMPLICATED.
BUT CHOOSING BETWEEN TWO HEARTS IS IMPOSSIBLE.

RUNNING HEARTS BOOK TWO

SAFFRON BLU

BLURB

Two rockstars.
One gorgeous girl.
Three hearts on the line.
What could possibly go wrong?

Matthew Dalcin, bass guitarist of Running Hearts, knows he let 'the one' slip through his fingers. So, he's elated when he finds himself falling hard for a beautiful soul that crosses his path. The last thing he expects is for his first love to step back into his life and turn his world upside down.

Finding love in the arms of a rockstar was never something Samantha Delany imagined would happen. When one rockstar leads to two, she wants nothing more than for them all to be happy.

William Sibree has been living with regret and a broken heart for far too long. So, when fate throws him back into his ex's life, he knows he can't stand back and watch his love walk away once again.

But if one heart is running scared, will two be enough to fight for what they know is right?

Rockstar love is complicated.
But choosing between two hearts is impossible.

Please note that Saffron Blu is Australian so there will be Aussie-isms in this book.

This book was tricky to write due to it being set in both Australia and America. It has has been written mainly in US English, but in an effort to keep some of the Australian characters authentic there are Australian words and slang in the chapters that contain their POV.

If you have any questions please don't hesitate to contact Saffron.

Some souls belong to together.

CHAPTER ONE

SAM

MY EYES FLICKED around the crowded arena cafeteria as I listened to my friend's panicked tone through my cellphone while I held it tight to my ear. "Sammy, I'm telling you I'm fucking lost. I can't tell you where I am other than in a nondescript abandoned corridor."

Aimee had a habit of stressing out, and I needed to bring her out of that so she'd think clearly. "Okay, stop and breathe. We'll figure this out. The band isn't going to be on stage for another twenty minutes, so we have plenty of time to find you." Spotting a handsome guy in a security vest, I let out an excited breath as an idea struck me. "Oh, I've got an idea. Hang on."

Holding the phone to my chest, I ran toward the security guard, but before I could get close, he disappeared through a door. I tugged on the handle to follow him, but the fact that it had one of those code locks on it halted my chase. *Fuck.*

I thumped my fist against the door and instantly regretted it. It was one solid door, and my hand was throbbing.

I pulled the phone back up to my ear. "Hey, you still there? Aims?"

There was a clattering sound through the phone, and I couldn't help but wonder if Aimee had dropped the phone or something. She was a clumsy bitch and always did crap like that.

"Fuck!" The voice wasn't Aimee. I knew that for certain because it was distinctly male, and it sounded distant, so I couldn't help but assume they hadn't picked up the phone. "She's out cold."

"Are you sure she isn't dead?" another male voice asked.

"*Aimee!*" I screamed through the phone, not caring as people around me stared like I was crazy. I needed whoever was on the other end of that call to fucking hear me and tell me what the hell was going on. I let out a loud whistle before screaming some more. "Oi, fuckers. Pick up the phone."

Then I repeated the process, and after what felt like a lifetime, a voice finally sounded in my ear. "Hello?" Relief flooded through me, knowing someone could finally tell me what was going on. "Oh, thank fuck. Where's Aimee? What happened?" I asked, desperate for answers.

"She walked into a door and blacked o—"

I cut him off. "I know Aimee's blonde, but she wouldn't just walk into a door."

"It was a freak accident, my buddy opened it, and she walked into it. There's an ambulance on the way, and someone has gone for some ice," he stated, concern evident in his voice.

"Where are you?" I asked, agitated to get to her.

"In a private corridor. I don't know how she managed to get in here. Where are you? I'll come find you."

"She was lost. I'm in the cafeteria. Fuck. You'll never find me in here. It's packed," I admitted as my stomach turned with panic flowing through me.

"There's an emergency exit in the far back corner of the cafeteria. Can you see it?" the male voice questioned.

Spinning in a circle, I quickly spotted the door with the bright green light over it. "*Yes!*"

"Wait next to that door, and I'll meet you there. What's your name, and how will I know you're who I'm looking for?"

I headed straight for the door, wanting to get there as soon as possible. "I'm Sam. Stay on the line, and I'll be the girl looking worried with a phone to her ear."

The sound of his laugh down the phone had my lady parts tingling. "Good point. I'm Matt, and I'll be the guy with a phone to his ear."

Standing by the door, I was searching the crowd for anyone who could be Matt. His breathing in my ear was comforting, knowing at least if we ended up in different places, we could still talk, and I'd manage to find Aimee. God, I hoped she wasn't too badly hurt. To be blacked out from walking into a door must have meant she'd hit it pretty hard.

The door beside me popped open, and I turned to find Matt Dalcin staring back at me. *The* Matt Dalcin. He was part of the band we'd come to see, and I briefly wondered who was watching over Aimee? *Jesus*, she'd freak if it were Saxton.

"Sam?"

I gestured to the phone in my hand. "That's me, and you're definitely a Matt."

He nervously rubbed at the back of his neck with his hand. "Erm… yeah. Sorry, I wasn't sure if you were a diehard fan and would freak if you knew. I didn't really want to come out to a million screaming girls. I—"

"It's fine." I cut off his rambling excuses. "So, where's Aimee?"

His eyes widened. "Shit. Sorry. This way."

He held open the door, and I stepped into the corridor while disconnecting the call and slipped the phone into my pocket as I followed behind him. I couldn't stop my eyes from checking out his ass. *And what a fine ass it was.*

"How much further?" I asked.

He slowed his pace until we were walking side by side and glanced down at me. "Just around the corner." He lifted a hand and pointed at the one coming up.

The instant we turned the bend, I spotted Aimee lying on the floor with someone crouched beside her. The sound of her laughter had my panic easing slightly. She couldn't be too badly injured if she were laughing.

As I got closer, I could see the bruising and swelling that was already coming up on her face, and it made my stomach churn. "Holy fuck! Aimee, are you all right?" My tone was calm, and I started to feel distanced from my body. I couldn't help but wonder if I was going into shock at the sight of her.

Matt's hand brushed against the small of my back, and the touch grounded me, bringing me back to my normal state.

"I'm okay as long as I don't move," Aimee stated, her voice laced with pain.

I crouched down beside her, and to give me space, the guy next to her moved away to stand beside Kat, the only girl in the band. Only in that moment did I recognize him as Saxton, the lead singer and Aimee's current celebrity crush.

The bruises on Aimee's face looked awful, making me wonder if there'd be any permanent damage under all that swelling. "Jesus, Aims, your face is a mess." I flicked a glare in the direction of Saxton, knowing he had to have been the *buddy* Matt had been talking about. Aimee closed her eyes and winced, clearly battling the pain, making my concern come back tenfold.

"Aims?" I whispered, unable to keep the worry from my voice.

"I feel like I've been hit by a truck." She was breathing shallowly.

"She's just up here," a new male voice announced, drawing my attention away from Aimee.

Two paramedics stepped up, crouching down beside Aimee. I stood and stepped away, giving them room. Matt's fingertips brushed against mine as he took my hand in his, the gesture a surprising comfort.

One paramedic gently pressed at Aimee's face. After a few minutes of assessing the rest of her body, the older of the two got up and strode back to the equipment they'd left a few feet up the corridor.

"Aimee, do you think you'd be able to stand and make it to the stretcher?" the younger paramedic asked her.

Aimee seemed to take a moment to access her body. "I guess I could try," she stated, obviously uncertain.

She slowly lifted herself into an upright position. Saxton and the young paramedic both grabbed an elbow as they helped guide her to the stretcher.

I watched as she relaxed back and let out a shaky breath before giving Saxton a grateful smile. "Thanks."

"Don't thank me. I'm the idiot who opened the door right into your face. I'm so sorry about that, by the way." He shook his head and seemed to wince as he took in her swollen face. I couldn't blame him, it looked so painful.

"Do I look that bad?"

"You look awful, Aims," I said, stepping up to her on the other side of the stretcher.

"Who's coming with us? There's only room for one," the older paramedic asked as his partner pumped the stretcher higher after lifting the safety rails on either side.

"That'll be me," I stated.

"You will not. If I have to miss the concert, you better take a million photos and record all my favorite songs," Aimee demanded, the panic audible in her voice.

I looked at her as indecision battled deep inside me.

"I'll go with her," offered the guy who'd brought in the paramedics. "I know you'll want to be kept in the loop since you'll be paying her medical fees," he added, his eyes on Saxton.

"I… no, I can pay them myself," Aimee demanded, her usual self-sacrificing self. I knew she didn't have the money to pay any medical bills, let alone ones that the kind of damage she'd received would rack up.

Saxton brushed a strand of hair off Aimee's face. The intimate gesture had me flicking my eyes away from the pair. "I caused this. At least let me pay to fix it."

I must have missed her agreement because Saxton spoke again. "Great. So, it's sorted. Sam's going to record your favorite songs for you, and my brother, Alberto, is going to accompany you to the hospital and give them all my details so that they can send me the bill." He looked to his brother, who nodded his agreement before eventually turning his attention to me.

I huffed, annoyed that he'd hurt my friend and was thinking he could erase the guilt by paying for her bills. Don't get me wrong, he should be paying the bills, but I don't think he should feel any less guilty because of that. The tension in my shoulders slipped away as I agreed. "Fine." I nodded at Saxton and dropped my eyes to Aimee. "So, that means you want every song recorded since they're all your favorites," I stated, trying not to show my anxiety about leaving her to go to the hospital with only the company of a stranger.

"Yep, but you love me too much not to do it," Aimee mumbled, her face probably hurting with every word.

I rolled my eyes. "Ugh, you're right."

Matt slipped Aimee's phone into my hand. Getting an idea, I turned to Alberto and passed it over to him. "It's Aimee's phone, I'm Sam. You text me the minute the doctors tell you anything." I made sure my tone was insistent and hoped he'd heard the threat hidden behind my words.

Alberto nodded. "Sure thing." I watched as he walked alongside the stretcher as the paramedics wheeled my best friend away, hoping I'd made the right decision in not fighting her and staying behind.

Matt wrapped an arm around my shoulder. "She'll be okay. Come on, I'll get you settled in backstage."

———

WATCHING Saxton rise on the stage from the position Matt had left me in was amazing. I couldn't help but wish Aimee was there with me. I quickly glanced at my cell, hoping to see a message from her or Alberto, even if it was just to let me know the doctors were checking her over.

I felt so guilty being there without her, but I also understood her insistence I do just that. I'd feel exactly the same if the shoe were on the other foot.

"Hello, New York!" Saxton called into the microphone, and the crowd went wild, cheers and whistles coming from all directions. "I want to take a moment to send some well-wishes to a lovely girl who should've been with you in the audience tonight. Aimee, this show is for you!"

I internally squealed at how sweet that was. Aimee was going to freak out when she finally got to watch the recording. She'd be playing that bit over and over again I was sure.

As the show went on, Saxton serenaded the audience. No matter how much charisma Saxton had, I couldn't seem to tear my eyes away from Matt and the way his muscles shifted in his tight shirt as he worked at his guitar.

Every sly glance he snuck my way sent a roll of excitement through me.

I'd thought he could've been flirting with me earlier, but I didn't know if that was simply how he was with all the girls. Every time he came offstage for a costume change, he kissed my forehead as he passed or stroked a hand over my shoulder, seemingly caressing some fire deep within me because I kept burning up with every tender touch.

The questioning look Kat kept throwing my way made me think he didn't usually act this way, which, in itself, sent even more excitement through me.

Once he was back on stage, I wiggled in my seat under his heavy gaze until it shifted to a frown over my shoulder, causing me to turn to check out what he was looking at. A short woman, looking to be in her early thirties, wearing a beige pencil skirt coupled with a matching blazer, was standing a few feet away, giving me a death stare. I didn't know what she thought I'd done, but it had to be something equal to selling off her first-born.

With a quick straightening of her skirt, she stepped up, stopping beside my chair. She didn't make eye contact, merely looked out at the stage as Saxton sang one of his sweeter ballads, and I let my eyes fall back there as well.

"They don't need a distraction like you and your friend, not when they're at the start of their careers. Saxton's song-writing ability will have them producing hit records for as long as they want. They could be one of the greats if they want to be." With those words of wisdom, she walked away, leaving me frowning after her.

Clearly, she had us mixed up with someone or something else because Aimee and I were not distractions. The guys had met us just over two hours ago. What made her think we had any control over their future?

"Good night." Saxton's words pulled me from my confusion, and I jumped off the chair as the three of them ran off the stage toward me.

Matt pulled me into a hug. He was hot and wet with sweat, but I didn't care. After all his little touches, I wanted him plastered all over me.

Saxton grabbed his sister, swinging her around in a circle, eliciting an excited scream from her. It was good being privy to this private moment, although I couldn't help but wish, once again, that Aimee was here to witness it as well.

The crowd erupted into chants, clapping and stomping feet. Matt let me go and guided me back to my seat. "We better go give them that encore. I'll be back."

The three of them did a three-way fist-punch thing before walking back onto the stage. I glanced at my phone and found nothing from Aimee.

Ten minutes later, they were all coming back offstage. Saxton disappeared behind the changing screen they'd all dressed behind between songs at some point during the night.

"Fuck!" he called before stepping out shirtless, a clean top held in one hand, his phone in the other. "We've got to get to the hospital."

Panic engulfed me. "What's happened?" You know when someone goes as white as a sheet? Well, I felt it happen to me. I felt the blood drain from my body. Matt stepped up beside me, grabbing my hand and giving it a gentle squeeze.

"It says they've put her into an induced coma." Saxton's voice was full of emotion, and I couldn't care what that might mean.

All I could think about was that one word — *coma.*

My best friend was lying in a hospital bed, alone and in a coma while I'd been enjoying myself at a concert. At that moment, I hated myself.

I was aware of people talking and Matt's arm over my shoulder, guiding me through corridors, but I couldn't see through the fog that had descended on me. I needed to see

Aimee, to speak to her doctors, and make sure she was going to be okay.

Because any other outcome was incomprehensible.

I couldn't imagine a life without my best friend in it with me.

CHAPTER TWO

MATT

Sam was shaking under my arm, and I pulled her in closer to my side, wondering if the cool night air was partly to blame or if worry for her best friend was the culprit. I wished I could do something to help bring back the outgoing person I'd met earlier, but deep down, I knew the only thing that would wash away the shocked and scarily quiet Sam would be to have Aimee out of danger.

Dom slipped into the back seat of the car, and I guided Sam to follow. "We'll be there in no time," I promised, not really knowing which of the two I was trying to comfort. Walking through the corridors, I'd been focused on Sam, but my best friend was clearly being eaten by guilt. I knew him well enough to see that — clear as day.

I made a mental note to keep a close eye on not just Sam but Dom too. I couldn't let him fall apart over this. He needed to keep his head straight because we had an album to write, and we couldn't do that if part of the team wasn't in the here and now.

By the time we stepped up to the hospital's reception desk

and requested information about Aimee, it felt like a much longer journey than it actually had been.

Whispers of Running Hearts could be heard, and I didn't miss the young nurse checking Dom out as she directed us to a private waiting area.

She blushed when she noticed my eyes on her and cleared her throat. "Someone will be out here shortly with information for you."

Sam slipped from under my arm and charged for Alberto. "What the fuck did you not understand about texting me the minute the doctors told you anything?" She shoved his chest. He remained silent but flicked his eyes to Dom's over her shoulder. "Don't look to him for help. Speak." Seeing the fire in her eased my heart a little, even though I couldn't help but feel sorry for Al.

Al sighed and rubbed a hand over his face before dropping into the nearest seat and focusing on Sam, who was still hovering over him, her arms crossed over her chest. "The doctors made it clear they were doing everything they could and you rushing here missing the concert..." His eyes flicked to Dom's. "Canceling the last concert of the tour." He shook his head. "It wouldn't have done anything to help Aimee. It would've simply given you more time to freak out and worry. I'm sorry, but I thought it was what Aimee would want. She wanted you to stay at the concert. That's why I was here with her in the first place."

Sam let out a furious grunt. "Don't you dare pretend you know what Aimee would want."

She stormed toward the red door, but before she got close enough to reach the handle, it opened, and a middle-aged guy in a white coat stepped into the room, closing the door behind him.

"I've been told you're Aimee's family," he started, his eyes taking the four of us in.

Dom threw his ball cap on the magazine-covered table in the middle of the room, and I stepped up to Sam, brushing my hand across the small of her back to ensure she knew I was close by.

"Mr. Saxton, I'm Dr. Kris Petrov," the doctor called, offering his hand to Dom as he carried on. "I've been treating your wife."

Dom's eyes were like saucers at the doctor's words, which I'd have found comical if I weren't so surprised by them myself.

The doctor's eyes briefly fell on mine as they worked their way around the room before falling back on Dom's still wide eyes. "She *is* your wife, right? Because unless you're immediate family, I can't tell you anything."

Sam smiled and offered her hand to the doctor. "Hi, I'm Sam, Aimee's life-long best friend. I was maid of honor, so I know they are husband and wife." She grabbed Dom's hand, and I felt a pang of jealousy at how easy it looked. "Mr. Saxton here was just a little surprised because it's a secret for the time being. The newlyweds have been able to enjoy the privacy that his fame doesn't always allow."

I was impressed with how quickly Sam reacted, not to mention how believable it was. If I didn't know better, I'd have believed her every word.

"Of course," the doctor said, making it sound like he understood, but I didn't care about his thoughts enough to take my eyes off Sam.

"So… my wife? How is she?" Dom asked, only stumbling over the title a little.

I listened along as the doctor explained how they'd put Aimee in an induced coma, which under the circumstances, was the best thing for her, never once letting my gaze leave Sam. I didn't know if she could feel me watching her or not, but her eyes flicked to me several times. When they connected with mine, I gave her a reassuring smile, hoping it would give her strength.

"When will she wake up?" Sam asked, the worry evident in her voice. One of her hands was still wrapped around Dom's, the other one seemed to be fidgeting with something on the hem of her top.

"Well, that's something we don't know. Everyone is different. Best case… a couple of days," Dr. Petrov announced, the uncertainty behind his words not reassuring one bit, and I could only imagine how worried that made Sam. If it were Dom the doctor was talking about, I don't think I'd be able to appear as outwardly calm. Sam's hand squeezed Dom's, and if I weren't watching her so intently, I don't think I'd have picked it up.

"And the worst case?" Dom asked.

"A few weeks."

Sam gasped at the doctor's admission and dropped Dom's hand before pacing the small room. "Aimee is strong. She'll be okay," she muttered to herself as she ran her hands through her long brown hair.

She quickly turned her attention back on the doctor. "When can we see her?"

Dr. Petrov's eyes scanned the room before he answered, "As soon as we have her in a private room, I'll send a nurse up to get you. You'll only be able to see her two at a time, though."

Dom thanked the doctor, who then rushed from the room as if he couldn't escape quickly enough.

"What the fuck were you thinking?" Dom yelled, his attention on Al as he stormed across the room toward him.

Sam dropped into the seat where she was and closed her eyes as she rested her head back against the wall. Knowing she probably felt lonely stuck with a group of strangers while one of her loved ones was in serious condition down some corridor somewhere, I decided she might appreciate some company and comfort. I walked over and sat beside her.

"I wasn't. The paramedics assumed you were her boyfriend, and I just ran with that. When I filled out the paperwork, I ticked husband, thinking boyfriend probably wouldn't be enough to get the information," Al stated, his tone making it obvious he felt bad about things.

Dom sat opposite him looking exhausted. I felt sorry for the guy because I knew even when he left the hospital, he wasn't going to be sleeping. This whole situation would weigh on him until Aimee was well and heading home. "You do realize there's going to be a shitstorm once the press gets a hold of this."

Sam didn't acknowledge that I was there, even though I knew she'd have felt me since all the seats were connected, and when someone sat in one, they all rocked a little. I stretched my legs out in front of me and placed my arms on the armrests, my elbow brushing against hers as I did so.

"It might not even get out. The hospital isn't going to say anything. They won't want the corridors full of paparazzi," Kat stated from the corner of the room, reminding me she was there. I'd been so focused on Dom and Sam on the way here that Kat had slipped my attention.

"I'm not worried about the press turning up here. I'm more worried about word of my *secret marriage* getting out," I heard Dom admit.

I hadn't taken my eyes off Sam, and I could all but feel her anger pulsating out of her beside me. "There's no fucking marriage. It'll be nothing more than a rumor. Aimee's up there, strapped to God only knows how many machines and all you care about is the press getting information on you that could harm your career. You're the reason she's up there, and if I didn't need you to get information from the doctors, I'd have kicked you out by now."

"I couldn't give two shits about my career. I'm more bothered about them harassing Aimee when she wakes up and tries to get back to her life," Dom yelled across the room, Sam's assumption having clearly bothered him.

It wasn't like I blamed either of them, really. All Sam knew about Dom was that he was a famous rockstar, and anyone would expect him to only care about himself, but I knew Dom, and she was so wrong. The guy I knew would put anyone he thought deserved it before himself, and seeing how he'd been with Aimee, she was more than deserving in his mind.

CHAPTER THREE

SAM

A WHOLE TWENTY-FOUR hours passed with nothing but quiet time spent at Aimee's bedside. With every puffing sound the ventilator made, I wanted to curl into a ball and cry.

Aimee was my best friend. She had been in my life for so long, and we may live continents apart, but I wouldn't know how to get through the days without hearing from her. I talked to her more than I did my own family most days. She was laid right before my eyes, yet I missed her. I missed her silly gif messages and sexy men's photos.

"Hey, why don't we go back to the hotel? Some sleep would probably do you good," Matt suggested. My eyes flicked to his across the room, and the sympathetic look he gave me made me wonder how bad I must look.

Alberto and Kat had both gone home not long after we'd arrived, knowing there was nothing they could do, and we'd only been causing chaos in the waiting area as people started to recognize the Running Hearts' band members. Initially, we'd been told there could only be two people by her bedside, but Matt refused to leave. Sitting outside her room had a similar effect that the band had in the waiting room, so the nurses caved and allowed him in too.

I frowned as I watched Aimee for a few seconds. "I don't want to leave her alone. If you're bored or tired, you're more than welcome to leave." I flicked my eyes to Dom. "That goes for you, too."

Dom slid down in his chair, seemingly settling in. "I'm good right here."

"Sam, you're shattered. You need to sleep, so you can be strong for when Aimee wakes up." He gave me a pointed look. "Besides, the doctor said she'd be out for at least a couple of days, so she won't even know you're gone."

I was exhausted. A dull headache was throbbing right behind my eyes, and I knew the dizziness I was feeling was also because of the lack of sleep. I ran a hand over my tired eyes and released a sigh of defeat. Matt was right, I'd be of more use to Aimee when she woke up if I was well-rested.

I pierced Dom with a demanding stare. "You promise you'll ring when you want to leave?"

"Sam, I swear I'm not going anywhere. And I'll call Matt if her condition changes at all." He seemed genuine in his promise, and he'd done nothing in the time since we'd met to make me doubt his word, so I decided to put my trust in him.

"Okay." His shoulders seemed to relax at my agreement, and I suddenly saw how tired he looked. "Make sure you take the nurse up on her offer of bringing a bed in for you so you can get some sleep, too. You look about as tired as I feel."

Matt stood and patted Dom on the shoulder. "She's right, bud. You look fucking awful."

Dom let out a short, sharp laugh. "So fucking charming, thanks."

Standing, I checked the time on my iPhone only to see the black screen reminding me it had died while I was talking to Aimee's mum not long after speaking to the doctors when we first arrived. I made a mental note to update her once I got back to the hotel and managed to get some charge into the thing.

"We'll be back in a couple of hours," I stated.

"It's midnight, and you might as well get a good night's sleep. Come back in the morning or, even better, lunchtime, if you can manage to sleep that long. Your body will need it," Dom suggested before flicking his gaze to Matt. "Can you give Al a ring and ask him to bring me a bag of stuff… clothes, toiletries, and a charger for my cell?"

"Sure thing. Are you ready to go, Sam?" Matt asked as he stopped by the door.

I followed him out the door and fell into step beside him as we made our way to the exit. He pulled his cap down low on his head, and it did a good job of hiding his face.

"Are you worried people will spot you?" I asked, curious about his answer. I'd never thought about how much fame would affect everyday life before but having witnessed the chaos the three of them being in the same waiting room caused earlier, I have a feeling it happens more times than not.

"I'm not bothered about the fans recognizing me. In fact, I love giving them autographs and posing for the odd impromptu photo. It's more that if the paparazzi are out there and see us, they may try harassing you, and that's the last thing I want." He gave me a quick side glance before dropping his eyes back to his feet once again, clearly trying to hide his face even more.

"We can always walk apart, so it doesn't look like we're together. You know, two random strangers exiting the hospital at the same time," I offered, dropping back a few steps.

He slowed his pace and grabbed my hand in his. "That isn't at all what I meant. We aren't walking out of here as strangers."

I stared down at his hand as we started heading for the entrance once again, wondering why he'd stayed with me and now was leaving with me. I knew his friend was also at the hospital, but they'd both only known Aimee and me for a few minutes when she'd been hurt, and they'd both—Dom and Matt—seemed to have taken us under their wings immediately. Hell, even Alberto had, having gone to the hospital with Aimee in the first place. It felt like we'd luckily stumbled upon the most caring people in America.

I braced myself for an onslaught as we stepped out of the main doors, but other than a couple of guys with cameras chatting near a parked van, there was no one to be seen. The guys barely glanced in our direction, and Matt made sure to keep walking, casually slipping his arm over my shoulder as he tugged me into his side.

The temperature was cool, and I was grateful for Matt's warmth against my body. I'd been running on adrenaline earlier in night, and to be honest, I couldn't remember if it was warmer or cooler. Hell, it could've been snowing, and I don't think I'd have noticed.

It didn't take us long to walk to the hotel. Luckily, we'd been booked in one close by the hospital, although I'm sure it wouldn't have been hard to find a cab at this time of night.

I veered us toward the elevator as we stepped into the hotel lobby, and Matt paused our progress. "Wait, I need to go and book a room."

I bit at my lip nervously. "You're welcome to Aimee's side of the bed since she isn't using it. It saves you spending money on a room when there's an empty spot there." He looked at me with an expression I couldn't quite decipher. "I promise I'll behave." I gave him a wink, trying to make him smile, and it worked.

Matt laughed. "It's more that I'm wondering whether I can behave."

I nudged him in the ribs. "I've taken self-defense. I'm pretty certain I can handle you." It was a lie. I was bone-tired and knew I wouldn't be able to fight off an ant, let alone a fit, six-foot-three man.

As the elevator doors closed on us and I pushed the button for our floor, our eyes clashed, and something crackled between us.

Standing perfectly still, my mind went blank as all I could think about was his arm brushing against mine.

CHAPTER FOUR

MATT

THE FEEL of Sam's arm against mine was branding me, and I knew I'd be able to feel the sensation long after she stepped away. My eyes bored into hers, asking for things I shouldn't be asking for.

God, I wanted to kiss her.

Needed to kiss her.

I'd only known the woman beside me a few hours, but I had no doubt I wanted to get to know her better. There was something about Sam that drew me in, capturing my attention. Even in an arena full of screaming fans, I couldn't stop my eyes from drifting to where she sat at the side of the stage. My performance tonight was all for her, not the thousands of fans who filled the stands.

My gaze followed as she pulled her lip in with her teeth. *Was she feeling the same things as me?* I reached out and popped Sam's lip free with the edge of my thumb before I even realized I was moving. I should've pulled my hand away immediately, but it was like it had a mind of its own. I ran my thumb across the edge of her plump lip and found myself leaning in.

Our lips connected, and I didn't know or even care who

closed the distance. All I was concerned about was the taste of her minty lip balm on my tongue and the scent of her floral perfume.

Sam's hands fisted my shirt as she seemingly tried to pull me closer.

The elevator pinged and the doors opened, then we quickly broke apart. Sam's face was aflame as we stepped out into the corridor, and I found myself relieved to find it deserted. I wouldn't want her to be more embarrassed than she already clearly was.

I followed silently behind, wondering if it would be best to head straight back down and book a room of my own because as much as I wanted to taste more of her, I wondered if that was what she needed right now.

Sam pulled her keycard out of her phone case and let us into the hotel room. As we stepped into the bedroom area, Sam turned toward her suitcase and started rummaging through it. "I'm just going to get changed," she stated before dashing into the bathroom.

I watched the door close behind her and strolled through the room. I noticed the two tidy suitcases and wondered whether the girls were living out of their bags or if they were planning on leaving sometime soon? *Would I even have the time I wanted to get to know her?*

I stopped in front of the big window and drew back the curtain just enough to take in the view of the city lights. I glanced up to the sky, knowing I wouldn't see the stars I was looking for because even though it was the early hours of the morning, there were still plenty of glittering lights—after all, a city never really sleeps. Being a country boy, I missed the dark countryside nights when you could look out any window and see all the stars in the sky. It was a sky you'd never see from the city.

"The bathroom is yours if you want it." Sam's voice had

me jumping out of my skin. I hadn't even heard the door open. "Sorry, I wasn't being quiet on purpose."

I gave her shoulder a gentle squeeze as I passed. "I was in my own little dream world. I probably wouldn't have even heard a train come rolling through."

When I stepped back into the bedroom after doing the bathroom necessities, the room was in semi-darkness, only lit up by a single bedside lamp. There was a small lump in the bed, so I headed around to the empty side. "Are you sure it's okay for me to sleep here?" I asked as I lifted the edge of the sheet.

Hearing no reply, I called her name a little louder. "*Sam!*"

"Hmm…" she muttered sleepily.

"Are you still okay with this?"

Sam huffed and snuggled down into the covers more. "Not if you're going to keep talking. I'd kinda like to sleep at least a little."

I chuckled, loving the fact she was full of sass even when she was sleepy. Having no change of clothes, I decided to sleep in my boxers, grateful I didn't have any ridiculous superstition about wearing the same lucky pair for every show. You'd be surprised at how many performers had a superstition like that. We featured a rapper, Darius, on one of our songs, and he went as far as wearing them for performances *and* recordings. That was a year ago, and they were in a terrible condition then. God only knew how he'd manage to wear them now.

After dropping my jeans and pulling off my t-shirt, I slipped into the bed beside Sam and tried to stay as still as possible, not wanting to disturb her any more than I already had.

Five minutes passed before Sam turned in the bed to face me. "Jesus, Matt. You're so stiff. Relax." She shuffled closer to me, and I automatically lifted my arm to make room for her. Once her head was resting on my pec and her fingers were spread across my stomach, I felt my body relax. As if the skin-on-skin contact had my mind easing, my body relaxed, which was odd because it wasn't like I'd had a sleeping partner recently. Even my occasional one-night stands always left immediately after the act, so my body shouldn't have been expecting to curl up against someone or crave the touch of skin like it seemed to be.

"Better?" she asked quietly.

"Much." I closed my eyes and smiled as I listened to the sound of Sam's breaths turning to a gentle snore. I was glad she seemed to be having no trouble finding sleep, even though I knew she was extremely worried about her friend. My mind wandered to Dom, and I hoped he'd managed to lose some of the guilt and find enough peace to sleep where he was at the hospital. Before I shook off all my concerns and enjoyed the feel of the soft, warm body pressed against me, I drifted off to sleep.

CHAPTER FIVE

SAM

A CELLPHONE RANG, and my pillow shifted beneath me. Only after a few seconds did I realize it wasn't a pillow but a body.

Matt Dalcin's body.

As everything from the previous day came tumbling to the forefront of my mind, I lifted myself off him and gave him the room to move, knowing from the sound it wasn't my cellphone. "You need to answer that, it could be about Aimee."

Without question or complaint, Matt reached for his phone, making me wonder if he'd already been awake before the noise started. "Al."

He shifted on the bed and quickly sat up before running a hand over his dark hair, leaving it sticking up in all directions. "Shit! I was meant to leave you a message last night. Dom wanted you to take him some clothes, toiletries, and a charger for his cell. It was almost dead last night, so that'll be why you can't get a hold of him now."

The room was still dark apart from the thin line of light shining under the door from the hallway, giving me no indication of the time. Suddenly, worrying about having slept too long and Dom not being able to call, I grabbed my phone to check the time.

Ten in the morning. That meant we'd had a good eight hours of sleep, and suddenly thinking about Aimee still lying in that hospital bed had me feeling the need to get freshened up and head back over there to see how she was doing. I could live in the hope that we'd maybe turn up to some good news.

"Okay. We'll be grabbing food and heading over there, so we'll probably see you there."

I frowned at Matt's words, not wanting to waste time grabbing food. I wanted to do the bare minimum—get showered, dressed, and brush my teeth.

Matt gave me a pointed look as he carried on talking to Al. "Yep, we'll take some food for Dom. I know he won't have left Aimee's side all night, not when he made the promise to stay."

Knowing we weren't going to get to the hospital as soon as I'd like, I decided the quicker I could get out of here, the closer I'd be to finding out how Aimee was, so I grabbed the first clothes I could find, not caring if they matched or were even clean and dashed into the bathroom.

By the time I came out, Matt was sitting on the end of the bed dressed in the clothes he wore yesterday since he didn't have anything clean to change into.

"Al's gonna bring some of my stuff to the hospital, too," Matt stated clearly, having read something on my face.

"Does that mean you're ready to go?" I asked, hoping his answer was going to be yes.

Standing, he gestured toward the door. "After you."

I didn't bother taking anything for Aimee because I knew I'd easily be able to pop back here if she were awake and needed anything. I secretly hoped that not preparing for her to be awake would give us some good juju, and then I'd turn up to find her awake and complaining I didn't have any of her stuff. Like it would jinx us but in a good way.

———

AIMEE'S ROOM was quiet when I entered, just the hissing of the machine breathing for her. My heart sank in disappointment at the sound. I'd really thought she'd be up and complaining about being stuck in the bed, all for a little bump on the head. My eyes ran over her body and stopped on her face. It looked worse than it had the previous night, which I'd not even thought was possible. The bruising was darker, and the swelling seemed bigger.

There was a rustle at the side of the room that caught my attention, and my eyes landed on a sleeping Dom. He was curled up on a rollaway bed that looked way too small for a grown man. Grabbing a chair from the edge of the room, I placed it beside the side of the bed, so I could reach Aimee's hand. She may not know I was there, but if I held her hand, I'd like to think she'd felt it, even if she weren't in a state to react to it.

Fifteen minutes passed with just the machines' noise and the rustling of the sheets as Dom tossed and turned on the small bed. The door suddenly opened, and Matt strode into the room, the smell of burgers following him. I'd managed to persuade him to drop me off on the way to the burger bar because it'd be best to eat here since he wouldn't want Dom's burger to go cold while we ate ours.

"Hey, who's ready for food?"

Dom jumped upright in the bed, sleepy, unfocused eyes roaming around the room. "Is she okay?"

"It doesn't look like there's any change. But I haven't seen a nurse since I got here, so I can't say for sure."

"You have burgers?" Dom's eyes lit up as his gaze fell on the bag in Matt's hand.

"I do, and one of them even has your name on it."

Dom grinned. "I could fucking kiss you right now."

Matt laughed and reached into the bag before throwing a burger toward Dom. "I'll pass on the kiss. Eat!"

Matt passed me a burger before dragging his chair across the room without caring to be quiet about it.

A nurse charged into the room and glared at him. "This is a quiet ward! We have patients who need their rest."

I hid my smirk behind the wrapper of my burger as I caught sight of the affronted look on Matt's face.

"Sorry, ma'am," he muttered as he unwrapped his burger.

My attention turned to the nurse as she fiddled with the machine and noted some numbers on the chart at the end of the bed. "Is she doing okay?"

"She's doing as well as can be expected under the circumstances." Her words didn't sound convincing. It seemed like a well-rehearsed line she said to most people regardless of the patient's condition.

"The doctor will be here for his daily check in the next hour or so. He may be able to tell you a little more then," the nurse stated as she headed to the door. "There are already more people in here than are normally allowed." Her words went quieter as the door closed behind her, but we still heard the other person's reply.

"I'm not staying. I am just dropping a change of clothes off for your patient's husband."

"Be quick," was all the nurse said.

The door opened, and Al walked in, looking only a little brighter than any of us did. Clearly, he'd not gotten much sleep himself, even though he had no connection to Aimee. "Kat sends her well wishes. It took me forever to talk her out of coming, too. Can you imagine the hassle of all three of you here… again? And in daylight hours this time."

Dom nodded as he scrunched up his burger wrapper and threw it in the open bag on the floor beside Matt's feet. "Thanks. I'm not leaving the room, so I shouldn't be spotted."

"Mom is going to go nuts if you don't go home with us."

"I'm not leaving until Aimee wakes up and kicks me out herself. So, Mom will just have to wait," Dom stated, the sincerity in his voice convincing me he was maybe a nicer guy than I'd given him credit for.

Aimee's hand twitched beneath mine, and I jumped up excited. "Oh my god! Aimee?"

Dom jumped up from where he was sitting and hovered at the other side of the bed.

"Her hand moved," I stated.

"Should I get the nurse?" Al asked, his hand already poised against the door.

"No. I freaked out last night when her hand moved under mine." His gaze locked on mine, and a look of guilt gleamed in his eyes. My eyes widened at his admission as I wondered why he'd held her hand if there was no one here to see. "The nurse said it could happen a lot before she finally wakes, and it's just her nerves."

Suddenly feeling deflated, I sat back down in the seat.

"Here." Matt held a water bottle out toward me. "You need to keep hydrated. I'll go grab us all a coffee in a little while."

My body practically melted hearing that word in anticipation of the feelings that will flow through me on that first mouthful. I hadn't even realized I'd not had my morning coffee yet, but having heard the word, I'm well and truly ready for it. "Coffee… yes, please."

"I threw a heap of your clothes in here, not knowing how long you'd be here. Toiletries, too. I'll take the rest of your stuff home with us. Kat's packing it all up now," Al informed Dom as he passed him a bag. His gaze fell on Matt. "Here's your change of clothes. I assume you'll be going back to the tour bus to grab your gear, or do you want me and Kat to take it with us, too?"

Matt glanced my way, and I gave him an uncertain look, not knowing what he was expecting to see to provide him with his answer. "Yeah. I'll grab my things later. They won't take it away until it's empty of our shit anyway, so I'm fine with leaving it there. Another day or two won't matter. Besides, it'll give Janice one last thing to stress over."

Day or two. Matt's words ran through my mind, and I was suddenly overwhelmed by a sinking feeling in my gut. Aimee and I were supposed to be flying out two days after the concert, which meant I needed to call the airline and rearrange our flights before it was too late.

CHAPTER SIX

MATT

I watched Sam's demeanor change. She suddenly placed her food down and started to scroll through her cell as if she was on some kind of a mission.

"What's wrong?"

"We're meant to be flying home tomorrow." Her gaze flicked to mine for a split second before she focused back on the screen before her. "Aimee obviously won't be making the flight, and there's no way I'm leaving without her, so I need to call the airline to rearrange our tickets."

I could see the panic riding her. Reaching out, I placed my hand over her forearm and gave it a gentle squeeze. "I'm sure they'll be understanding. It's a medical emergency, after all," I said, hoping to reassure her.

Sam stood. "I've found the number. I'm gonna head outside, I'll be back soon. Hopefully, I won't be on hold for too long."

"Finish your food first."

She shook her head as she strode toward the door. "No. My stomach's churning. I need to get this all figured out first. Otherwise, I'll just feel like shit."

"I'll walk out with you. I need to get back to Kat," Al stated as he followed behind Sam, who'd not bothered to stop and wait for him, clearly not caring whether he joined her or not.

I didn't like her answer, but it wasn't like I could force her to eat. If she really was that worked up, food on top of that would simply leave her with an upset stomach. I watched the door close behind them before tearing my eyes away to find Dom grinning at me.

"What?" I asked, regretting the question immediately because I could tell he had his teasing head on.

"You really care for her."

I frowned at his statement. "I could say the same to you." I gave him a knowing look. I understood he felt guilty about causing Aimee's injuries, but I knew him well enough to see that wasn't what was keeping him here.

"Fair point."

"And I could say that I at least have spent time with Sam to justify caring. You spoke to Aimee for what, five minutes between her coming to and leaving in the ambulance?"

Dom gave me a pointed look. "We're talking about you here, not me."

I sighed, knowing I had to talk about it. I kept going over it in my head. Maybe talking it through with Dom would help me understand my feelings because even I thought I was acting a little crazy by caring as I did so quickly. "Fine. Yes, I do care for her. She treats me like a normal person. Like I'm not some big rockstar. You know as well as I do how endearing that is."

Dom laughed. "Tell me about it. I don't think anyone has ever given me a piece of their mind like Sam did last night."

I chuckled at the memory. "Everyone is too worried about losing us as clients to be blunt with us. And fans, well, they're just too overwhelmed with speaking to their idols that they can barely string a sentence together, let alone give you a good chewing out."

"She's pretty fucking awesome."

"Special. I think she's special. So yeah, I care." I glanced at the blonde in the bed. "So, what's going on in your head?" Because I knew something was, and I was certain it had to be remarkably similar to what was going around in mine.

Dom ran a hand through his hair and sighed. "It's crazy. Like you said, I spoke to her for all of five minutes, but in that time, no matter how short, I felt a connection of some sort."

I gave him wide eyes. *Was he talking about a love-at-first-sight thing?*

"Don't look at me like that. I admitted it was crazy." He rubbed his chin.

"They're going back, though, so it's not like we'll get to know them any better or…" *Or what?* I wanted so much more, and yet I barely knew the girl.

Dom was right.

It was batshit-fucking-crazy.

"Do you mind watching her while I go take a quick shower?"

I screwed up my face. "I'm not going to watch her like a creeper, but I'll sit with her while you shower."

Dom rolled his eyes as he grabbed the bag Al had left for him. "You're a dickhead."

CHAPTER SEVEN

SAM

As the cheery-voiced woman kept talking on the other end of the phone, my heart sank into the pit of my stomach.

"But I'm the only person she has here. I can't leave her to wake up in a foreign country alone," I argued, cutting her off mid-sentence, not wanting her to ramble on about the rules of flight changes.

"I understand, ma'am, but unfortunately, it's out of my hands. Because of your recent travel history, customs will not allow your flight to be changed. If you were immediate family, they may have overlooked it if we'd set you up with a new return flight, but they won't see your 'sisters from another mister' as immediate family like you do."

I bit back the argument on the tip of my tongue and forced myself to take a deep, calming breath, knowing no matter what I said, the outcome wouldn't change. The next day I'd have to leave my best friend in a hospital bed while I flew back home.

"Okay. I'll be at the airport tomorrow."

"Good. I'll email you with the steps you need to take

regarding changing Aimee's flight. Is there anything else I can help you with today?"

I wanted to laugh at the stupid question, considering she didn't actually help me in the first place, but it would be rude since it really wasn't her fault. She was sticking to the rules and script she was trained to do and say, so I replied with, "No, that's all. Thanks." I spat the parting word because, in my opinion, she'd done nothing to warrant the thanks I was giving her.

"Have a nice day," she sang before ending the call.

Sliding my phone back into my pocket, I looked up at the blue sky scattered with fluffy white clouds. It was a pleasant day, and I soaked in the sunshine, sending up a little prayer that Aimee would wake up before I'd have to leave.

Dom had been willing to hang around for her, but how long will that last? If she didn't wake up for another week, would he still be there? And when she did wake up, what would that mean for her? Would she have to stay alone in a hotel until she got the okay to fly? Or would they keep her in the hospital? Again, all alone.

I undid my too loose ponytail and pulled it back up tighter before turning and heading back to Aimee's bedside.

Matt turned in his seat as I stepped through the door, and a wide smile lit up his face. He must have seen something in mine because it dropped in an instant. "Not good news?"

I shook my head. "They can't change my flight."

The bathroom door opened, and the scent of soap and men's deodorant filled the room as Dom stepped through the door looking freshly showered. "I can buy you another ticket," he offered, clearly having heard me through the closed door.

"Thanks, but it won't matter. I've done a lot of traveling in the last few months… Germany to Australia, Australia to here. It seems to have caught someone in border security's eye. They are pretty much demanding I leave on my flight, or they'll probably come looking for me."

Aimee's phone on the tray table started ringing, and I rushed across the room to grab it, not wanting to miss a call from Aimee's family. They'll be worried enough about her as it is, they don't need to worry more if they can't reach me.

"Hey!"

"Sam, how is she?" Sarah's concern was more than obvious in her straight-up question.

"She's stable but still unconscious. The doctors aren't sure when things will change, but they don't seem overly concerned."

Sarah let out a sigh of relief. "That's good. If they aren't worried then that's really good."

"Yeah. There's one problem, though. I can't change my flight and have to leave tomorrow."

"Okay…"

I waited for her to finish, but it seemed like she didn't have any ideas either. "I don't want to leave her alone." A hand slipped into mine and gave it a gentle, comforting squeeze, and I knew without looking it was Matt. I didn't know how I'd become so lucky to have had him here for me throughout this, but I know I'd have been such a wreck if I hadn't.

"She won't be alone," Dom stated. "Not for a second."

I tore my eyes from Aimee and locked them with Dom's determined stare.

"I promise you, Sam. I'll stay here with her for as long as it takes."

I believed him. He meant every word. The thoughts I had earlier come back to mind. "What about when she wakes up?"

"I'll stay until she tells me otherwise. Okay?"

I nodded.

"That boy sounds like he has a heart of gold," Sarah stated in my ear.

I laughed. "I'm not sure he'll appreciate you calling him a boy."

"Pfft… he's a boy to me. Put me on speaker, so I can thank him for everything he's doing for my daughter."

I pulled the phone away from my ear and did as she asked. "You're on speaker, Sarah."

"Young man, I want to thank you for being there for my daughter."

"Ma'am, you don't need to thank me for anything. I'm to blame for your daughter being here in the first place. I'll never be able to make up for that."

"Sam, do you think I should fly out, so I can be there for her."

"Honestly, I think she'd rather know you're looking after her boys while she can't. We both know how much she hates leaving them in the care of her douche of an ex." I felt at peace knowing I was right in what I'd said. That's exactly how Aimee would feel.

Sarah chuckled. "That's very true."

"Ma'am, I don't know if you heard me tell Sam, but I'll tell you the same. I promise I'll stay with her for as long as she needs me to." Dom's eyes darted to Aimee as a haunted look crossed his face. "I'll be here at her side until Aimee says otherwise."

"Oh. I wouldn't make promises like that. Our Aimee doesn't have it in her to kick someone out. You'll be stuck by her side forever if you wait for her to tell you otherwise." We all could hear the smile in Sarah's voice and how proud she was of her daughter being such a wonderful person. And being Aimee's best friend, I knew Sarah had a good point because Aims would never make someone leave if they said they wanted to stay.

"Well, I guess you might be getting a new son-in-law then," Dom joked.

Matt chuckled beside me, and Dom flicked his eyes to him questioningly. "Actually, isn't that kind of already the truth since everyone here thinks you're her husband?"

Lighthearted laughter filled the room, and even though Aimee wasn't conscious, it lifted our spirits. I hoped if it were true that coma patients could hear what was happening around them, it was lifting Aimee's spirits too.

CHAPTER EIGHT

MATT

WE'D STAYED in Aimee's room for most of the day before I'd managed to talk Sam into leaving, so she could get a decent sleep before her flight. *Our* flight. I'd already been on with the airline and managed to book Aimee's now-empty seat. It didn't feel right to leave Sam to travel alone when she was still extremely worried about her best friend. I just hoped she saw me going with her as a good thing.

I watched her dash around the hotel room making sure to grab all her last little bits. She'd packed Aimee's things first, and Alberto had already dropped by to collect them. He'd driven down in Dom's car so he could park it at the hospital for when Aimee woke up, with his dad following behind. Aimee's bags would be handy in the trunk for when she'd need her stuff.

"That's the third time you've checked that drawer. And I bet you didn't even put anything in it to begin with," I told her, wondering if she had a touch of OCD.

Sam sighed but relaxed at my words. "I know. I don't think I ever opened the drawer before this morning. I just don't want to leave anything behind."

I stepped over and pulled her into my arms. I smiled into her hair as she came willingly. "Worst-case scenario, the maid will find whatever you leave, and they'll be in touch. Dom can even pick it up, and Aimee can bring it home with her."

Sam nodded and breathed deeply against my chest. The warmth of her breath was easy to feel through the thin material of my t-shirt. "You're right. Thank you." She stayed in my arms for another minute, nothing but the sound of our breaths filling the room. It was calming, and I loved having her pressed against me. It felt right to have her in my arms. She finally stepped back, and I released her, knowing we couldn't stay there all day. "Let's go. I have a flight to catch."

Sam grabbed her backpack, and I threw my large overnighter over my shoulder before wrapping my hand around the handle on her suitcase. I still hadn't told her I was going with her. I kept telling myself it was because I wanted it to be a big surprise at the airport. But the real reason—I was worried that she'd tell me she didn't want me to go with her.

We'd taken an airport transfer the hotel offered, and thankfully, we hadn't needed to share it with anyone else. I'd been pretty lucky not to be recognized in the hotel. I'd hung back while Sam checked out and organized the transfer, so nobody managed a close look under my cap. But I knew if someone had sat with us on the minibus, there'd be no avoiding being recognized. Truth be told, I was a little concerned about the flight and how many people might recognize me on there, but we'd be stuck in the air, and it's not like they could alert the press. Well, with planes having Wi-Fi these days, I guess they could alert them. That would mean we'd arrive to an army of paps waiting for us, but I'd worry about that later. Nobody would cause problems on the flight, at least.

We stepped up to the check-in desk, and Sam offered the lady her passport and ticket. I watched as they went through the process of loading her suitcase on the scale before shooting it along the conveyor belt.

The airline lady smiled at Sam. "Here are your boarding passes," she said as she handed the little cards over.

"Thank you." Sam turned toward me, and I could tell she was ready to direct me away, but I quickly stepped up to the counter.

"Hi, I'd like to check-in as well, please." I could feel Sam's eyes boring into me, but I couldn't turn to look at her because the woman had asked for my passport and was glancing curiously between it and me.

Her eyes widened when she'd finally recognized me as one of the members of Running Hearts. She cleared her throat and nodded. "Of course, sir."

She typed into the computer in front of her and flicked her eyes to mine, a blush covering her cheeks. "Have you got any luggage you'd like to check-in?"

My eyes fell on my overnight bag, and I tried to remember what I had in there and whether there was anything I'd want to take out and use on the flight. I crouched down and quickly pulled out my phone charger and earphones before placing it on the scale. "Just that, thanks."

While the woman was busy with my bag, Sam caught my attention by tapping my arm. I hadn't dared look at her in case I saw rejection in her eyes, but I locked onto her chocolate-brown orbs, relieved to see them glistening with tears and a wide smile plastered across her face.

"Thank you." She pressed her lips against mine and all too soon pulled away. "I'll put those in my backpack if you'd like?" she offered, nodding toward the wires hanging loosely in my hands.

I handed them over as the woman behind the counter offered me my boarding passes. I took note of the seat number and relaxed, seeing the number next to what I'd noticed printed on Sam's. There hadn't been any last-minute changes that had separated us for the flight.

After slipping my passes into my pocket, I wrapped my hand around Sam's and led her away from the counter toward the security section so we could get settled in the departure lounge. Sam pulled me to a stop in a relatively empty area beside the toilets, and I glanced down at her.

"Everything okay?"

She frowned at me like she was working out a ridiculously hard math equation. "Why?"

I raised a brow. "Why, what?"

"Why did you get a ticket?" She gave me a flabbergasted look like she shouldn't have had to explain that.

"I couldn't let you go just yet. I want to spend as much time with you as possible." Feeling like I'd maybe said too much, I quickly went on, "Plus, I've heard Australia is beautiful, and I haven't had a holiday in a long time."

Sam gave me a sly grin, making it clear she knew it had nothing to do with Australia being beautiful. "Come on, then, let's get through security and relax before our flight," she stated, slipping her hand into mine and tugging toward the line of people waiting to go through to the departure lounge and gates.

CHAPTER NINE

SAM

I FLICKED my eyes to my left and watched Matt sleep for a minute, his head resting against the side of the plane. I couldn't quite believe he was right there next to me, all because he wanted to get to know me more. He spouted something about Australia being beautiful and needing a holiday, but I knew that was a last-minute add-on to feel less vulnerable about laying his reasons out. He made it pretty obvious.

I didn't want to leave Aimee in America, but I'd be lying if I didn't admit she wasn't the only reason I wanted to stay. I wanted to spend more time with Matt. I liked him a great deal, and I felt an undeniable spark between us that I wanted more time to explore. The kiss we'd shared in the elevator was playing on my mind, and I was dying to taste his lips again, but I didn't dare make the first move in case he didn't feel the same. I'm a chickenshit, and I know it.

"Is that who I think it is?" the girl beside me asked. She'd been quiet most of the flight, but I'd caught her glancing at Matt several times during the twenty-two-hour flight, and clearly, she'd plucked up the courage in the last hour.

I turned my attention around and took her in. She looked to be in her late teens and most probably a huge fan of Running Hearts, so there was no point denying it. I nodded. "I think it might be."

"My friends are never gonna believe I sat next to Matt Dalcin." She gave me a sheepish smile. "Well, almost next to him." She pulled out her phone. I guessed it was to send a message to her friends, and I quickly placed my hand over her phone.

"Would you mind waiting until we've landed?" I gave her what I hoped was a pleading look. "Otherwise, there'll be an army of fans and paparazzi waiting for him at the arrival gate."

Her eyes widened in surprise. "I didn't even think about that." She nodded and placed her phone back on the tray table. "It can wait."

I sighed in relief. "Thank you." I glanced back across at Matt. "I'm sure Matt wouldn't mind posing for a selfie and giving you an autograph once we land, too."

"Oh my god! Really?"

I nodded, hoping I wasn't offering something Matt wasn't willing to give. I'd seen him happily pose for selfies when he'd been recognized in the hotel once or twice.

She grinned and bounced in her seat, obviously unable to contain her excitement. "That would be amazing. By the way, I'm Shelly."

I took her offered hand. "Sam. Nice to meet you, Shelly."

Our conversation was cut off as the pilot spoke through the speaker, updating us on the local time, weather, and our upcoming descent.

I nudged Matt beside me. "Hey, sleepyhead..."

He cracked an eye and trained it on me. "Are we there yet?"

I smiled in amusement. "Almost. We should be landing in about twenty minutes."

He groaned and stretched in his seat, his shirt lifting and flashing me a delicious peak of his abs. "And then we have to get on another plane."

"The next one is only an hour and twenty minutes long. I'm sure you can handle it." I patted his thigh in mock sympathy.

Matt placed his hand on mine and gave me a warm smile.

I turned my hand over beneath his and linked our fingers.

"I might just make it."

———

MATT GAVE Shelly an autograph and selfie as I'd promised. Nobody else seemed to pick up why—they'd made it look like a couple of friends taking a quick snap—so we made it on the next flight and to our final destination of Brisbane without any delays.

The closer I'd gotten to our destination, my mood seemed to sour. I wasn't looking forward to driving to Aimee's parents without Aimee. She should be there with me getting hugs from her kids.

"Are you okay?" Matt asked, squeezing my hand gently as we walked out of the airport and toward the long-stay parking.

"I will be when Aimee wakes up and comes home." I twisted the hand I was using to pull along my suitcase to catch sight of my watch. "Could you ring Dom and see how Aimee is?" I asked since it wasn't too late in New York just yet.

Matt pulled out his phone without question or argument. Butterflies took flight in my stomach as I stood listening to his side of the call.

"Hey! Yeah, we just landed in Brisbane. Sam was wondering if there's any news?" Matt bit at the corner of his bottom lip while listening to Dom's response. I wished Matt had put it on speakerphone, but I knew it was best not to with them being celebrities and everything.

"Okay, I'll let her know. Get some rest, and I'll call you on the flip side." Matt slipped the phone in his back pocket and his hand back in mine before proceeding to tug me along the pavement.

"Well?" I asked, unable to wait any longer. I suddenly felt sick, wondering why it was taking him so long to tell me what Dom had said. *Could the doctors have given him some bad news?*

If I had left the country, and Aimee had fallen into a more dangerous state, I'd never be able to live with myself.

CHAPTER TEN

MATT

I GLANCED at Sam as she drove us to Aimee's parents' house. I'd planned on booking myself a hotel, but she'd insisted there'd be room, and it wasn't like I would mind sleeping in her bed with her.

I couldn't believe how well we'd hit it off. It was as if we'd had some magical connection over the phone when I was trying to find Sam and bring her to Aimee.

Don't get me wrong, Sam had been extremely worried about her best friend, but she'd not been able to stop giving me sneaky glances and blushing every time I caught her looking. I didn't know if she realized the fact I caught her meant I had been looking at her too.

I'd made it clear what I was feeling with gentle touches here and there, but it hadn't gone any further than that. Sam was too concerned to take it any further, and I didn't blame her one bit.

"She'll be okay, you know?" I stated, knowing she was once again thinking about her friend lying in a coma on the other side of the world.

Sam tucked some loose dark hair behind her ear. "I know. I just hate the fact that I had to leave her there."

Reaching out, I placed my hand on her knee, causing her to flick her eyes my way. "I know you don't trust him, but Dom will look after her."

Sammy gave me a quick smile before returning her attention to the road. "I sure hope so." She didn't sound convinced at all, but we both knew there wasn't anything she could do to change the situation. Sam was here, and Aimee was with Dom in New York.

I wished I could ease her mind, but she didn't know Dom, not really. She knew what the media showed him to be, and honestly, some of that wasn't always good stuff. In fact, a lot of it wasn't great. The real Dom, my best friend, was a good man with a huge heart, who I knew, without a doubt, would do everything he could for Aimee while she was still in America. Hell, knowing Dom, I wouldn't be surprised if he'd be in her life for a hell of a lot longer than that.

Sam pulled the Mini Cooper onto a pebble-dashed driveway, parking it between what looked like a Chevy Colorado —only it had a badge that wasn't Chevy on it, most probably Australia's version of that—and another Mini Cooper. I could tell both Minis were different models since the one we were in seemed longer in size and blue than the one we were parking next to being red.

"You guys like Minis?"

Sam laughed. "Yeah, to Spencer's dismay, Aimee's dad," she clarified, obviously noticing my questioning gaze. "He's a mechanic and insisted that parts are super expensive for them, but sadly, that didn't sway either of us from buying something he didn't approve of."

Three kids rushed at the car around the side of the house, and Sam's face lit up as she hurried to get out. "Boys!" she greeted them as they all seemed to throw themselves at her in a mass group hug. I laughed as I exited the car, drawing the attention of a woman who looked to be in her early fifties and had just rounded the house.

"Hi, I'm Sarah. Aimee's mum."

I took her offered hand in mine, squeezing it gently as I gave her a warm smile. "I'm Matt. It's nice to finally meet you. I've heard a lot about you from both Sam and Dom. Dom's my brother in every way except by blood."

"Ah, just like Sammy and our Aimee." Sarah smiled, looking over at Sam. "Family by choice."

I nodded. "Exactly." It wasn't like I didn't love my own family, but we weren't close-knit like the Saxtons. I was blessed the day they chose to bring me into their family because they taught me what a real family was like, and I wanted nothing more than to show my own kids the love shared with me.

"I miss Mummy," the youngest boy said as his chin wobbled.

Sam dropped to her knees in front of him and placed her hands on his shoulders, holding him at arm's length to look him into his eyes. "I know, sweetie, so do I. As soon as she wakes up, she'll be on the phone to you, and the minute the doctors let her fly home, she'll be here, giving you all the hugs she can. So many hugs you'll be begging for her to stop."

"I'll never ask her to stop," the little guy said adamantly.

Sam stood and tugged on the boy's hand. "Come on, do you think you have the muscles to help me drag my suitcase into the house? Matt over there is a total weakling. You should've heard him complaining when he pulled it to the car from the airport."

The boy ran a wary eye over me.

"She's totally lying," I said, hooking a thumb in Sam's direction.

Sam gave us both wide eyes faking mock astonishment. "I

never lie," she promised before throwing a wink in the boy's direction. He let out a belly laugh as she dropped his hand and opened the trunk of the car.

I reached in and lifted the case out before she could, making sure to pretend it was extra heavy as I did. I figured I might as well play along.

"See. So weak," Sam whispered conspiratorially in the boy's ear, making him chuckle again as he pushed the suitcase across the drive and toward the front door, where a gray-haired man, who looked to be around five-foot-seven, was waiting.

Sarah pulled Sam into a hug, both ladies had watery eyes, and I turned away to lift my backpack out the trunk before closing it, hoping to give them both what privacy I could.

"This is Matt," Sam offered as the two broke apart, gesturing to me.

Sarah offered me a warm smile before turning back to Sam. "We met when you were talking with Dan."

"Oh, okay. I'm sorry I didn't warn you about having Matt with me, it was a last-minute decision."

"Actually, Dom told me as soon as Matt booked his flight. I haven't set him a bed up, though, because I didn't know if he'd be in your bed or not?" Sarah flicked her eyes between the two of us curiously.

I turned my attention to Sam, wondering what her reaction would be because I'd be lying if I didn't say I wanted to know the answer to that question too. Sam's face had turned the brightest shade of red I'd ever seen on her, and I had to fight back a smile.

"I can easily set him up a bed if I was wrong in suggesting anything else," Sarah stated clearly, thinking she'd been on the wrong track.

Sam shook her head. "No, as long as you're okay with it. We're under your roof, after all."

"You're both adults. Neither Spencer nor I will dictate how you live your lives."

"Thank you." Sam turned her gaze to mine. "Unless… you'd rather sleep in a room of your own?"

I gave Sam a soft smile as I stepped in closer. I slid my hand against her cheek and tilted her head back slightly before pressing a quick and gentle kiss against her soft lips. "I wouldn't want to be anywhere else but next to you."

"Aww. Both my girls have found their guys," Sarah crooned, her voice filled with emotion.

"I wouldn't get ahead of yourself, Sarah. Aimee and Dom haven't even had a conversation except for when she was concussed."

Sarah waved her off dismissively. "Pfft… I've seen that boy watching her when he FaceTimes me, and the look he has on his face tells me there's a connection there. Just as there is between the two of you."

Sam watched Sarah, her eyes wide in shock. She didn't even blink when Sarah turned on her heel and headed into the house. I slid my hand down Sam's arm and slipped it into hers.

"Are you going to show me our room, then?" I asked, trying to break her inner freak out.

CHAPTER ELEVEN

SAM

"I WOULDN'T WANT to be anywhere else but next to you."

Matt's words were running in my head on a loop. It was the most romantic thing anyone had ever said to me, and I was completely freaking out. *How could someone like him feel that way about me?* He could have the choice of any girl out there. *What does he see in little old me?*

I liked him a lot before I even met him, but as I was getting to know the real him, my feelings were becoming stronger. I couldn't help but think I wasn't interesting enough for someone like him to commit to someone like me. I was starting to worry that the more I got to know him, the closer I was getting to heartbreak.

The knowledge that I was going to share a bed with Matt was making me freak the hell out. It wasn't like I didn't want Matt to share my bed, but the last time we did, I hadn't had a chance to enjoy it. I was so exhausted and wracked with worry about Aimee, so doing it again in a better frame of mind was something I wanted. It simply scared me because it had been a while since I'd been with a guy.

After my last boyfriend, I'd taken time to find myself and

essentially fall back in love with the real me because somewhere along the way, I'd completely lost her and the love I once had for her. So dating again and being intimate with someone was a terrifying thought. I wasn't going to let it stop whatever was happening between Matt and me, though, because Sarah was right, there was some insane connection between the two of us that needed to be explored. I wanted to give us a chance.

I led Matt to *our* room, waving him in and closing the door behind us. As I glanced around the cozy area, I noticed my bed had fresh purple bedding on it and made a mental note to thank Sarah for making it up for me. The desk against the wall had a small pile of unopened mail and what looked to be a book delivery from Amazon. I wasn't in a rush to open anything, so I flicked my eyes over to the two floor-to-ceiling bookcases beside the desk and hoped Matt wouldn't be put off by my taste in reading material. There was a lot of gay romance on those shelves, and I didn't know how straight guys felt about that kind of stuff.

Matt dropped his backpack on my bed and walked straight over to the bookcases, running his fingers over a spine here and there. He stopped on the shelf that held the books written by me and pulled one out. It was my most recent release, a gay romance that I absolutely loved writing, so much so that I'd planned out a whole series and spin-off series for it.

His eyes raked over the cover—two half-naked guys in a loving embrace. "You wrote this?" he asked before flipping it over and reading the blurb.

I waited until his eyes came back to me before I answered, not wanting to disturb his taking in the words. "I did. Gay romance is a popular genre, and it's one I've loved for a long time as a reader and now a writer. The LGBTQI reading and writing community is welcoming to all, and it's somewhere I feel at home," I said, my voice sounding defensive even to my ears.

I couldn't help it, but in my experience when people found out you read or wrote LGBTQI romance, they assumed you were all kinds of kinky, but that was so far from the truth. Gay romance seemed so much more emotional to me because the obstacles the characters come across were often hard-hitting and just *deeper* than a lot of heterosexual romance books. Something about that spoke to me, and that was why I was drawn to them.

"Hey," Matt offered me a warm smile. "I didn't mean anything by it. I'm impressed that you're writing a genre you don't have personal experience in. It must be hard to do and require a lot of research."

"Sorry. Most people don't think that way." I gave him an abashed glance. "Yeah. I guess it's not as easy as writing heterosexual romance, where I can find inspiration from my own life experiences. The internet is full of inspiration for my muse, though, so it's not overly hard."

Matt chuckled as he slotted the book back into its place. "Well, I guess gay porn is easy enough to find."

Heat rose on my cheeks at how close to the truth he was. I'd spent many hours watching videos on a gay porn star's Twitter feed during the writing process—all in the name of research. We can't have sex scenes being unrealistic, can we? "I meant photos like the one on the cover and music. You'd be surprised how easily lyrics can spark a plot bunny, even if the song was written about a guy and a girl."

"I know the power of lyrics pretty well." He nodded. "Every time Dom hands me his lyrics, and I hear the melody in my head, I know exactly what chords will go where. I pretty much get lost in the process until I have a whole song."

"I didn't realize you guys worked together like that. Did it happen naturally, or did Dom choose to focus on the lyrics?"

I asked, curious about the process. Aimee and I have co-authored together, and we fell into our characters pretty easily, no arguments over who wanted to be the voice for who. I wondered if songwriting was similar.

Matt shook his head. "No, nothing was forced. Dom's always been better with words. He feels them just as I feel the music. I guess those differences between us are why we work well together."

Matt sat on the edge of the bed, leaning back on his elbows. Taking his cue, I toed off my sneakers and kicked them under the bed where they usually lived before lifting a pillow and sitting against the headboard.

"Kat and the others? How does it work with them? Do they not get upset that they don't get a part in bringing the songs to life like you and Dom?"

"Kat puts her mark on them. She's amazing behind that drum kit. I could never give them as good a beat as she does. Al used to be our keys player, and our old school buddy, Will, was a bass guitarist, but they both left the band for personal reasons when we were signed, and we've never managed to replace them with anyone permanent. We usually just get new guys who learn the songs for the tour."

My eyes widened with his admission. "Alberto was part of the band?"

Matt nodded. "He's a fucking whiz on the keys."

"He's not someone I can imagine in the limelight."

Matt grinned. "He hated the attention fame was bringing, and that was before we even really hit it off. He didn't want to lose his privacy or put the kind of pressure that brings to his future relationships." He frowned. "I guess maybe he's the smart one out of the band."

"What about the other guy? Will, was it?" I played with a loose strand of cotton between my fingers as I watched the thoughts behind Matt's eyes, unable to read into them.

When I thought he wasn't going to answer, he opened his mouth. "Will was…" He laid back and looked off to the ceiling, his eyes unseeing as a small smile graced his lips, "… more than simply an old school buddy. He's my soul mate. Dom, Will, and I were like triplets, completely inseparable. Dom noticed girls before we did, and that started it all, I think." Matt blinked and turned his head to face me. "Anyway, when we were signed, it was clear how the record company wanted to present us, and Will didn't want to be someone he wasn't, so he chose to step away and focus on his love of art. He's a tattoo artist and now owns his studio back home in Cold Spring." There was a sadness in his voice that urged me to hug him, but we were too far apart for that.

Reaching across the bed, I placed my hand on his shoulder and squeezed it. "I bet it was hard losing that connection all of a sudden." Worry flashed in his hazel orbs. "You said you were pretty much inseparable, so I'm assuming once you were signed, you were whisked away to do music stuff, and he was back home living a life you were no longer a part of," I clarified.

CHAPTER TWELVE

MATT

My heart hammered in my chest until Sam explained her comment. I thought I'd let more slip than I'd meant to. It wasn't like I didn't want Sam to know everything about my life and friends, it was just that some relationships were more personal than others, and as much as I felt for Sam, I wasn't sure I was quite ready to bare all to her just then.

I relaxed, turning on my side so I was facing her and linked my fingers with hers as her hand slipped from my shoulder. "Yeah, it was hard, but I kept busy, so I didn't really have the time to dwell on it. It probably wasn't anywhere near as hard as it was for you to move away from your family. How did you end up in Australia, anyway?" I asked, turning the subject to her, wanting to know anything she was willing to share with me. I wasn't lying back at the airport when I'd said I wanted to get to know her more.

Sam's eyes fell on our hands as she talked. "I miss them every day, but I've always wanted to see the world, and what better way to do that while getting to spend time with my soul sister." The smile she was wearing made it obvious how much she cared about Aimee. Although I'd already known that from how much she worried about her. "I FaceTime with my family regularly, and I plan to go back home for a visit next year. I spent a year in Texas as an exchange student at the age of fifteen, so I've spent time away from my family before." That explained her accent. I'd thought it had an almost American twang hiding behind the German.

"Technology is a wonderful thing. We all get to feel like we aren't too far from home via video messaging when we're on tour, too." It was nice connecting with Sam over similarities when we were from such different walks of life.

———

TAPPING on the door pulled me from the depths of sleep. I rubbed a hand over my face and smiled when I saw Sam's sleeping form beside me. She'd obviously changed her position on the bed after I'd dozed off, still in the same spot I'd been in with my legs hanging off the side of the bed.

Another tap came on the door accompanied by a feminine voice. "Sammy? If you guys sleep any longer, you'll be awake all night. Jet lag isn't nice. I've been there a few times."

I cleared my throat. "Thanks, Sarah."

"You're welcome. I'm making coffee if you want one," she offered.

"I'd love one, thanks." I stroked my hand over Sam's cheek. "Sam, you need to wake up. Do you want a coffee?"

She gave me an indecipherable grumble.

"I'll make her one. Sam never passes up her elixir of life," Sarah informed me. I heard her footsteps gradually fade away and focused my attention back on Sam, who didn't look like she was even trying to wake up.

"I'm awake," she mumbled, probably sensing my eyes on her.

I chuckled. "You don't look it. Your eyes are still shut."

"Okay. My brain is awake… just. My eyes are still asleep."

I smiled, thinking mine felt the same. Even though we'd slept for a lot of the journey from the US, it obviously wasn't a good enough sleep to keep us awake after chatting for a couple of hours. It was a great conversation that flowed easily, and the deeper I got to know Sam, the more I liked her.

"Coffee is on the counter," Sarah called out.

I stood and stretched, smirking as I noticed Sam's eyes trained on the patch of abs that my riding t-shirt flashed before taking Sam's hand and tugging her up. "Come on, let's get you that life elixir. It might wake you up."

"Elixir of life," Sam corrected. "And the way I feel right now, I don't even think that's gonna work."

Our drinks were on the breakfast bar, and we both parked our butts on stools in front of them, sipping our coffee in silence. It wasn't long before Aimee's youngest son joined us, jumping up on the stool beside me. "Hey, I'm Dan," he offered me his hand, his brown eyes locking on mine.

"Hi, Dan, it's nice to meet you. I'm Matt," I said, taking his hand in mine and giving it a gentle shake.

"Chris says you play guitar and sing. I had guitar lessons, but I liked the drums best until I broke my arm. I never sang."

I grinned. "I do. What did you learn to play? Maybe we could play it together sometime."

"Have you brought your guitar?"

Dan's question surprised me. Not because he asked it, but because I hadn't even thought about not having my guitar with me. It wasn't like I could've carried it to the airport with me without Sam asking questions, so the whole surprise of me joining her would've been spoiled. Dan must have seen something in my face because he laid his hand on mine and looked at me with solemn eyes. "It's okay, you can borrow mine or even my mum's."

I frowned. "Your mom plays guitar?"

"No, silly." He laughed. "She bought one to learn and never did."

"Oh. Well, that's a nice offer. I might just take you up on it if you don't think she'll mind." It probably wouldn't be top of the line like some of mine were, but my old favorite wasn't either—it was always the one I'd pick up whenever I reached for one.

"Chris, you've got to leave for your rugby game in ten minutes. Are you ready?" Sarah called out from the lounge.

"Yeah, Nan, I just have to get my boots." Chris walked out of what I assumed was his bedroom, and a smile spread across his face as he caught sight of Sam. "Hey, Sam, are you and your boyfriend going to come and watch me play? I know you still prefer American football over rugby, but come on, you've only watched a couple of games and not one of mine."

Sam's eyes fell on mine. "Would you mind?"

I glanced back at Chris, who was also watching me with a hopeful stare. "Are you kidding? I'd love to watch a rugby game, and if there's someone I even know playing… all the better."

"Did you say we have ten minutes?" Sam asked Chris.

"It's probably closer to five now."

She guzzled down the last mouthful of her coffee before sliding off her stool. "I'm just gonna freshen up. Don't leave without me."

CHAPTER THIRTEEN

SAM

IT TOOK me fifteen minutes to get ready, but thankfully, Chris's game was a home game and was being played on the local university fields, which were only a five-minute drive away. Chris and Sarah had left, but it was easy enough for Matt and me to follow in my car.

By the time we found Sarah in the crowd of parents along the sideline, the game had only just started. Spencer was the team's coach, so he was under the team shade tent, chatting to the kid who sat on the subs' bench. I ran my eyes over the field. Chris was easy enough to find on the right-wing. He gave us a little wave when he spotted us, earning him a telling-off from his closest teammate.

"I'm sure you're meant to distract the opposing team," Matt offered with a laugh.

I giggled. "I didn't mean to distract anyone."

The game seemed pretty fast-paced. The parents' shouting and cheering had me confused as to who was actually winning, though. There wasn't a scoreboard, and I hadn't thought to keep track of the numbers myself. Matt started to cheer along, and I thought he must have some idea about the game. I leaned into his side, so he'd hear me over the crowd and asked if he could explain the rules to me.

He laughed. "I have no idea. I'm cheering when Sarah gets excited."

At half-time, the kids huddled together under a shade tent and sucked on what looked like oranges while Spencer talked to them animatedly. The referees appeared back on the field, and at that point, the kids threw their hands together and let out a loud cheer before running onto the field ready, refreshed, and reenergized for the second half.

It went pretty much the same as the first half, except our team seemed to be running in the opposite direction. The only reason I knew Chris's team had won was because once the final whistle was blown, the whole team jumped, cheered, and ran at each other offering high-fives and hugs. It was such a great atmosphere. Even the opposing team high-fived the winners as they walked off the field, the team captain offering a cheer.

"Three cheers for the Crocs. Hip Hip…"

"Hooray," his team called.

He clapped, as did his team. "Hip hip…"

"Hooray"

"Hip hip…"

"Hooray."

Chris's team captain offered the same for them.

"Three cheers for the Hornets. Hip hip…" the team following through with the three cheers. It was such a great sense of sportsmanship, and I was really impressed.

"You wouldn't see that happening in an American school game," Matt said into my ear, his breath fanning over my cheek, sending goosebumps in its wake.

Chris's match had been the last of the day, and it was late afternoon by the time it ended. The temperature was still up in the mid-eighties, and it probably would be until well after sunset. Matt's phone rang, and he pulled it out of his pocket.

I gasped as my heart leaped into my throat at the thought that it could be Dom calling about Aimee.

Matt's eyes fell on mine after he'd taken in the name on the screen. "It's my mum," he told me. As much as his words eased my heart a little, I didn't think my heart would really ease until we did get the call from Dom telling us she was awake and coming home.

"Hello," Matt said into the phone. I offered him a smile and waved him away, so he could take his call privately. I watched his back as he strode across the field and away from the crowds of people celebrating the winners.

"He's a nice guy. I can see he cares for you," Sarah said from beside me. I flicked my eyes to her, surprised she was there. Last time I'd seen her, she was running into the middle of the field to hug Chris.

"I don't know if he cares, but he's a great guy."

"Dom is, too. I hope Aimee gets to know him before she comes home. It would be such a shame for her to lose the chance of knowing a good guy for once."

I smiled. That would be great. Aimee hadn't had much luck in the past with guys, and meeting a nice one for once was an experience she really deserves. "Yeah, I hope for that, too."

The douche canoe who was Aimee's ex-husband walked over and congratulated Chris and Spencer on the win. His eyes landed on me, and I forced a polite smile. I'd been Aimee's best friend for a long time. Even though I lived across the other side of the world for the majority of our friendship, I was there through their relationship and all of its troubles. I hated the guy in front of me even more than Aimee did.

"Any news on Aimee?" he asked.

"Nothing new," I offered, selfishly glad when I watched

his face fall in disappointment. Matt stepped up beside me, his arm brushing against mine.

Douche Canoe's eyes flicked to Sarah's. "I heard your place is getting a little crowded. If you need us to have the boys for a few days, we can."

"It's not crowded," Chris argued. "Sam's part of the family, and Matt's her boyfriend." I bit my lip in order not to smirk. Douche Canoe's hate for me was equal to mine for him, and it was nice to see him grimace as his son had my back.

"Thanks," Sarah said to the douche. "We'll keep your offer in mind, and I'll let the boys know it's there, but we're all fine at our place."

He nodded and chatted for a few minutes with Spencer and Chris about some of the plays during the game. I couldn't follow it, so I lost track of what they were saying after a few seconds and turned my attention to people-watching.

I loved to people-watch. It was a great way to spark my muse. You never knew what magic could happen from seeing a look pass between two people.

———

WE HAD a celebratory dinner when we got back to the house, Spencer firing up the barbecue, a beer in hand.

Reece came out of his bedroom and set up the pool table they had on the undercover patio. "Do you want to play, Matt?" he asked shyly, making me smile. Reece was the quieter of the two older kids, and it was nice to see him trying to come out of his shell. Aimee would be proud.

"I'd love to," Matt answered excitedly.

"I'll play the winner," I said before anyone else could. I'd lived in the house long enough to know if you didn't make a claim, you'd be sitting through three or four games before you got to touch a cue.

"Damn," Chris complained. "I'm after you."

After Reece's first few shots, Matt leaned against the wall. "Jesus, Reece, you're good at this. Am I ever going to get a turn?"

Reece laughed and got another one of his balls into the pocket. "Maybe," he said as he shrugged his shoulders.

Sarah brought out a portable speaker, and Chris chose an awesome playlist with songs from the sixties, seventies, and eighties for us to listen to.

The night was filled with good food, great music, and fun had by all. At some point during the evening, Dan brought out Aimee's guitar and asked Matt to play for us, which he happily did. Once he started strumming on the strings, you knew he was doing what he loved. His body seemed to relax, and his eyes closed as he opened his mouth and sang a beautiful acoustic rendition of one of their pop songs. It almost had a country feel to it.

A few hours later, just as we were ready to call it a night, Sarah's cellphone rang, and as soon as she caught sight of the name on the screen, she quickly answered, "Hello."

I watched with bated breath as she listened to whoever was on the other end of the call.

"Uh-huh… yeah, I guess no news is good news." She didn't sound happy about the admission, but it was the truth. Even if none of us were satisfied by the lack of news, we all simply wanted Aimee to wake up, and the more time that passed before she did, the more worried we became. I didn't think any of us wanted to voice it, but with each day that passed, I couldn't help but wonder if she'd ever come back to us. I was pretty sure I wasn't the only one thinking that.

"Thanks for calling, Dom. Look after yourself while

you're watching over my daughter." With a smile and a final goodbye, she hung up.

The kids had gone to bed an hour earlier, and Spencer stood after draining the last of his beer bottle. "I think I'm going to call it a night," he stated.

"Me, too." Sarah stood and grabbed her empty wine glass off the coffee table. "Night, guys."

"Night," both Matt and I offered in unison.

Once we were left alone and Matt's eyes landed on mine, there was a heat in them that had warmth pooling in my stomach. "Are you ready to head to bed, too?" His words were full of promise, and as much as I was excited to see where things would go between us, I was also terrified of falling too deep, too quickly. But I didn't care. Just like Aimee, I deserved a chance with a good guy, and I wasn't going to pass this chance up.

"Yeah," I answered, my voice sounding breathier than I'd intended.

CHAPTER FOURTEEN

MATT

SAM'S BREATHY reply played on my mind the whole time she was in the bathroom getting ready for bed. It was probably what gave me the nerve to pull her into my arms the second she stepped into the room wearing her tank and shorts PJ set. The shorts were black, covered in purple stars, and the matching black tank had a large purple glitter star across the chest and the words '*Shine Bright*' underneath.

She looked up at me, her palms relaxed against my chest. "Hi!" She pulled her bottom lip between her teeth, and all I wanted to do was free that plump lip and taste it. The second her lip popped free, I crushed my lips against hers.

Sam moaned into my mouth, and I took advantage of her parted lips by slipping my tongue inside, tasting her minty fresh breath. Her hands slid up my chest, and her fingers delved into the hair at the base of my neck.

I dropped my left hand to her ass and pulled her tighter against me, needing to feel more of her. I knew she'd be able to feel my hard-on between us, and when she lifted her leg, wrapping it around my thigh before grinding her pussy against me, I lost all my control. I hoisted her up, so she had no choice but to wrap both her legs around my waist and blindly walked us over to the bed, not breaking the kiss until I had to and placed her on the soft mattress.

Sam fumbled for the zipper on my shorts the second I released her. A smile took over my face at her eagerness, and I leaned back slightly, giving her the room to get to what she wanted. She pushed my boxers down along with my shorts, and my cock sprung free. Sam flicked her eyes to mine and licked her lips as a blush rose across her face. "Can I…"

Even though she'd left her question hanging, I knew what she wanted and gave her a brief nod. I'd never been asked my consent for someone to blow me before. It was always a given, but the fact that Sam was asking, surprisingly turned me on all the more as the appendage in question throbbed, and a drop of precum leaked out of the tip.

I groaned as her tongue teased the head, licking off the precum and then swirling around the ridge before her mouth opened wider, and she slid it down my shaft, engulfing my cock to the hilt.

"Fuck," I called out, trying to keep my voice quiet, knowing we weren't the only people in the house. The sight of her deep-throating my cock was erotic. Nobody had ever taken me in that quickly and deeply before.

Sam ran her hands up my thighs, her nails scraping along my flesh as her fingers curved around my ass, pulling me tighter against her face as if she couldn't get enough of my dick. I wanted to close my eyes and bask in the feeling, but I didn't want to miss a second of the sight before me—her plump pink lips shining with wetness while stretched around my shaft. She looked so fucking sexy.

She slowly slid her mouth back up my shaft and ran her tongue over the underside as she did. One of her hands left my ass, and she stroked the base of my cock. One pump, two pumps before she once again wrapped her lips around it and bobbed her head, following the rhythm of her hand. She hummed around my dick, and I couldn't hold off closing my eyes and dropping my head back as I basked in the sensations. Her other hand shifted from my ass cheek, and her fingers fondled my balls. I felt them tightening, and when she rubbed a forefinger over my taint, there was no holding off my climax.

"I'm gonna…" I slipped my hands into her hair and gave her a gentle tug in case she didn't hear my warning, but her eyes locked onto mine as she kept on greedily sucking my cock.

"*Sam!*" I breathed her name as I came. I watched her throat work as she swallowed it down and couldn't believe how uninhibited she was. I couldn't wait to have my turn tasting her, but first, I needed to sit my ass down because my legs were about to buckle.

As soon as my cock popped free from her mouth, I dropped onto the bed beside her, falling onto my back. My eyes closed as I focused on catching my breath.

I felt the bed dip and her arm brush against mine as she laid beside me. She giggled. "That good, hey?"

"Good? Fucking amazing. Epic. What's a word that's better than that because it totally was, and I can't think straight to find a suitable word. You just blew my mind." I turned my head to look at her. She was on her side watching my face, a huge grin across hers.

"They do say guys think with their dicks, so maybe I did just blow your mind." She fell into a fit of hysterics, and I couldn't help but laugh along with her.

If I felt like I could move, I'd wipe that smirk off her face and show her how it feels to be on the other side of a blown mind.

CHAPTER FIFTEEN

SAM

I GASPED as I tried to stop laughing. My joke wasn't even that funny, but I'd just sucked off Matthew Dalcin, and clearly, my brain decided now was a great time to freak out and fall into a fit of hysterics. Aimee would never let me live this down if I ever told her. The thought of her not recovering brought me back down to reality, and I vowed then and there that no matter what teasing Aimee gave me, I'd be telling her about my post blowjob giggle fest.

Matt shifted onto his side and ran a finger over the glittered star across my chest, making my nipple peak under the thin material, and all my concerns about Aimee drifted to the back of my mind.

"My turn to taste you." Matt's voice was huskier than normal, and it sent shivers of anticipation through me. His fingers lifted the hem of my tank, and I arched my back off the bed enough for him to easily strip me of it. I'd usually be shy and feeling vulnerable when in this position with a guy, but as I was bared to him, Matt revered me as though I was the sexiest thing he'd ever seen. Boy, did that do a girl's self-confidence a world of good.

Matt dropped his mouth to one of my nipples and licked over it with his tongue. My back arched off the bed as goosebumps broke out over my skin. He kissed his way over to the other nipple and showed it the same attention.

My breath came out in short pants as he kissed and sucked his way down to the waistband of my shorts. He paused and cut his gaze to mine, a question on his face. I lifted my ass off the bed in answer, and he slid my shorts and underwear down in one quick tug. He wasted no time, and once he had me bared, he spread my legs and swiped his tongue over my slit.

The warmth of his breath against my core and the feel of his tongue lapping at my lips had me moaning. "Mmm…"

He pulled his mouth off my pussy and grinned up at me. "You're so fucking sexy."

"Matt… less talking. More—" My words were cut off with a groan as he speared his tongue into my pussy. I couldn't help but move my hips in rhythm with his tongue, trying to get where I needed to be.

Matt's thumb brushed over my clit, giving me another sensation to pull me closer to the edge.

"Oh god. Oh god," I chanted before quickly placing my hand over my mouth to muffle my cries.

His tongue ran through my folds and circled my clit. While two of his fingers stroked in and out of my pussy, need pooled inside me as I climbed closer to my climax. His teeth nipped at my clit, and the pain-pleasure of it sent my orgasm crashing over me.

Matt's fingers left my pussy, and even though I'd come, it felt like a loss. I wanted more. I wanted him to fill me. I shifted up the bed with what energy I had left. "I want you, Matt. All of you."

Matt lifted his shirt over his head, and I finally got to see him in all his naked glory. I'd been so worked up in my need to get him off first and then climax myself, I hadn't realized he wasn't completely naked.

I let my eyes roam over him, the peaks and valleys of his muscles contracting as he rolled on a condom. He clearly worked out regularly to keep his magnificent physique, even though I hadn't seen him enter a gym in the few days I'd known him.

He smirked. "Like what you see?"

"Oh, yeah. If you come up here, I might show you how much," I said. Feeling somewhat courageous, I slid my hand down my body, stopping just above my mound as I let my legs fall open, so he could see how wet and ready I was for him.

"*Fuck!*" Matt cursed as he climbed up the bed and hovered above me, taking his weight on his elbows as his hands cradled my face. "You're so beautiful."

I crushed my lips against his, tasting myself on him and wondering if he could taste himself too. Just the thought of it turned me on all the more.

I felt the tip of his cock brush against my entrance. Before he ran it through my wet slit and up to my clit, I felt him reach my entrance again. Unable to take any more teasing, I wrapped my legs around the back of his thighs, not giving him the room to shift back again.

As a reward, his dick slowly inched inside me.

"You feel so good, Matt. So good," I moaned in pleasure as he stroked in and out of me.

Matt groaned. "So do you, Sammy."

The way he said my name with such reverence sent my heart beating crazily in my chest. *Could I dare to hope he was having feelings toward me like I was him?* Because as much as the thought of having feelings for him this soon terrified me, I had to admit they were there, even if I were only willing to admit them to myself right now.

Matt brushed his mouth over mine and ran his tongue

over the seam. I let him in without any hesitation. I wanted as much of him as I could get, as much as he was willing to give me. The way he devoured me, I had the feeling he was giving me everything he had.

One of Matt's hands roamed over my thighs and around my ass, his fingers squeezing my cheeks as he slid over it. I fisted my hands in his hair and tugged, pulling a grunt from him. For a second, I worried it might have been too much, but when he thrust faster and harder, the thought disappeared.

I met him thrust for thrust, gasping into his mouth as I got closer and closer to climax. *"Matt,"* I whispered his name against his lips as my orgasm washed over me.

"Sammy," I heard him whisper as his cock throbbed inside me, sending another shockwave over me before I fell into a blissful haze.

CHAPTER SIXTEEN

MATT

THE SOUND of kids laughing woke me, and when I glanced at the clock on the bedside table over Sam's head, I was surprised to see we'd managed to sleep through the night and even most of the morning. It was almost eleven o'clock.

"It's my turn."

"You just had your turn."

The boys' voices were easily heard through the door, and I momentarily wondered how much noise we'd made last night.

"I'll unplug the machine, and nobody will play on it," Sarah threatened them in return.

I chuckled, wondering if that were something Aimee would normally do. It was strange because although I hadn't really met her—except for a couple of minutes between her coming around from Dom knocking her out and her being wheeled away in an ambulance—I'd heard so much about her since that day that I felt like I knew her.

"What's so funny?" Sam's voice was husky with sleep, and the sound brought a smile to my lips as I pressed a soft kiss to her shoulder.

"Nothing really, just the kids and Sarah." I kissed my way

across her shoulder, and when she tilted her head, giving me more access, I made my way up her neck.

"Mmm…" Sam hummed, clearly enjoying my mouth on her neck. "What time is it?"

"It's probably just past eleven."

She jerked in my arms. "Holy shit!" Sam turned to face me and gave me wide eyes. "We slept in."

I nodded.

"Do you think we might ha—"

"Don't say it, you'll jinx us," I said, effectively cutting her off.

Sam pressed her forehead to my chest with a groan. "Oh, please don't tell me you're superstitious."

I let my fingers trail up her back. "I'm a musician, and superstition comes with the talent."

Sam's breath tickled my chest as she let out a laugh before pressing a kiss to the center of my chest. "Then, I guess I'll have to forgive you."

Sam stiffened as we heard Sarah's phone ringing in the other room. We both waited in silence, listening to see if it was news about Aimee. Dom's tinny voice was easy enough to recognize, but it was distorted enough that we couldn't decipher the words through the closed door.

Sam sat up and leaned over the bed to snag her pajamas and underwear off the floor before quickly tugging them on. Knowing how deep her concern for Aimee was, I followed her lead and pulled on my shorts.

Once we were out of the room, Dom's voice coming from the phone in the kitchen became much clearer. "No news is good news, right?"

"Let's hope so." Sarah sounded deflated, and I felt so bad for her. Her daughter was in a coma halfway across the world, and there was nothing she could do but wait. I knew from experience that waiting sucked.

"She'll wake up. I'm certain of it." Dom sounded so sure. If I didn't know better, I'd think he was psychic or something.

Sarah spotted us and smiled. "The sleeping beauties are finally awake." She glanced back at the screen on her phone and pressed her finger to the screen. "Wave to Dom."

Sam waved her hand, "Hey, Dom."

I also did as I was told. Sarah wasn't someone you didn't obey. I guessed it was something to do with her grandmotherly voice. "How are ya, Dom?"

"Ah, you know me, I'm good." He didn't sound convincing this time, and I started to worry that this was taking a toll on him. I hoped the guilt wasn't eating away at him. I knew it was bothering him before, and I could only assume the longer she stayed unconscious, the worse it would get. I made a mental note to call Al and ask him to check in on his brother.

"You do realize we can all tell that you're lying?" Sarah offered, calling him out. "You better be remembering to eat."

"I am, Sarah. The nurses bring me meals when they feed the patients. I think they worry they'll have another patient if they don't look after me."

"Good. You need to look after yourself because when Aimee wakes up, she'll need you to be healthy and running on all cylinders, and you can't do that if you've been starving yourself."

"I promise I'll be everything your daughter needs when she wakes up."

Sarah smiled at Dom. I saw a twinkle in her eyes and couldn't help but wonder what she was thinking. "I'm going to pass you over to Matt, so you guys can catch up. Thanks for calling, and I'll look forward to talking to you again tomorrow."

"You're more than welcome, Sarah. Catch you tomorrow."

Technology was brilliant. The fact they could video message each other across the world every day never ceased to amaze me. I accepted the phone from Sarah and turned it in my hand, grinning at my friend on the screen in front of me. Sarah was right to be worried about him, he looked like he hadn't slept for days.

"Jesus, Dom, you look like shit."

Dom chuckled halfheartedly. "Thanks. Way to make a guy feel good."

Sam walked around the kitchen counter and headed for the coffee machine. She glanced at me and mimed drinking while mouthing *'coffee?'* I nodded and offered her a grateful smile before turning my attention back to Dom to have a well-needed chat with my best buddy. I hoped, if anything, I could at least offer him a little distraction or company to get through what must be another long and draining day.

CHAPTER SEVENTEEN

SAM

THE SOFT GOLDEN sand beneath my feet was hot, and I had to pick up my pace to get down to the harder stuff that had been cooled by the water lapping against it all day.

When Matt had suggested a stroll on the beach to take our minds off our friends still in America, I figured we both needed it. The quiet rocky beach at Point Cartwright was the best place. There are never many people there, and although Matt hadn't been recognized over here yet, I was more than aware it was only a matter of time. And it probably wasn't far from Matt's mind either.

I tugged Matt closer to the shoreline, and we walked along the ankle-deep water in companionable silence, our fingers laced together between us.

"Have you ever been in love?" I asked. It was a question that had been playing on my mind a lot since getting to know Matt. He'd never really spoken about an ex, but whenever the subject of relationships came up, he either turned the subject my way or moved onto something else without answering me.

"Have you?"

There he went again. Deflecting.

"Ah-ah, I asked first."

Matt sighed. "Can we sit?"

I nodded, and he led me away from the water but only far enough to stop and sit on the start of the dry, softer sand.

"Yes. I was in love once. I was a kid and didn't understand that's what it was at the time, but looking back on it now, yeah, it was love." I could hear the pain in his voice, and although he said he didn't know at the time, it had clearly ended in heartbreak.

I glanced at him as I pulled my knees up and rested my head on them. "Tell me about her?" I spoke softly, hoping that he knew he didn't have to if he didn't want to. I had a feeling he needed to talk about her and the breakup, but I wasn't going to force him.

Matt ran his finger in the sand in front of him as he spoke, his eyes glued to the movement. The crease of worry in his brow had me watching him more intently, needing to look for any sign that I may be prying too much.

"He. It was a he." He turned his gaze to me, and the defeat that showed in the slump of his shoulders made it clear he didn't like what he saw in my face.

My eyes were so wide in surprise that my eyebrows had practically risen to meet my hairline. I quickly schooled my features. "Hey." I reached out and ran my hand over his thigh beside me. "There's nothing wrong with that. Like at all. I was just surprised. Tell me about him."

"He was my best friend." I couldn't stop my eyes from widening again, but this time he smiled at the sight. "Not Dom. At school, we were called the three musketeers… me, Dom, and Will." The name was said on a breath, and there was so much emotion attached to it. I was instantly grateful I'd brought the conversation up because he needed to get this out. He'd mentioned Will in previous conversations, but there was never that much emotion behind the name. I guessed he'd kept it buried deep until opening up to me at that moment.

I won't lie. My heart plummeted hearing it because even though I knew Matt liked me, I didn't think I'd ever be able to compete with memories of this person. *Will.*

Matt carried on talking, clearly not noticing my worries. "As I've said before, it was the three of us who actually started the band back in high school. Kat and Al joined us, and we got signed. Shit happened, and he didn't want us to live in the closet, but that's the only way we could be because the label made that perfectly clear in the contract." Matt shook his head sadly. "I'm sure we could've fought it if we really wanted to, and Will did, but I was a coward. I was too scared to have it any other way." Matt stared out to the turquoise ocean, and we both watched a bird dive for fish for a moment or two.

"Do you think you two will ever clear the air?" I asked, feeling the need to break the silence and get him back to talking before he decided he'd done enough.

He sighed. "Probably not. Our chance has gone, and any contact we have just brings up memories. Good. Bad. They all hurt." He spoke quickly like he felt as though the sooner he got the words out, the quicker the subject would be finished, and I started to feel bad about pushing him more. Maybe I should've just left him watching the bird.

"*Holy shit!* Look!"

I snapped my eyes up from the sand at the excitement in Matt's voice and let my gaze follow his finger. I frowned as I watched the water, unsure what he was looking at. Just as I was about to look away, a whale broke the water's surface, rising and crashing back down making a huge splash. "A whale." I flicked my eyes to Matt. "It's a freaking whale."

We both jumped up, keeping our eyes on the vast open water waiting for our big friend to pop up again.

"There." I pointed a little further up the beach than he had been last time, clearly making his way somewhere. I vaguely remember Aimee mentioning to me that it was whale-watching season, and if we headed to the beach when we got back from the States, we might just catch sight of some swimming down the coast, but never in my wildest dreams did I believe I'd actually see one.

Matt points to a grassy area above where the beach ends and a rocky cliff face starts. "I bet we'll get a better view if we go up there."

I grinned. "Race ya," I said as I ran up the beach.

"You sneaky cheat, getting a head start." The humor was clear in Matt's voice. I picked up my pace, knowing he'd have a much longer stride than me since he was a fair bit taller, after all.

Strong arms wrapped around me, and I was suddenly pressed against a hard chest. "Jesus, woman, I need a breather. Running on sand takes it out of ya."

I turned in his arms—grateful for the reprieve—and slid my hands up his chest, only stopping when I had them locked around his neck. "A breather, hey?" I gave him my most salacious smile.

He licked his lips, and I knew what was coming before he even leaned in. So when his lips covered mine, I instantly opened, allowing his tongue to sweep inside. I'd become addicted to his kisses during the time we'd been here in Australia. I'd been so worried about Aimee while we were still in America that nothing had happened between us there except that moment in the elevator. At the time, it wasn't something I was really aware of, but now I feel like it was wasted time, especially when I knew he wouldn't be staying here forever. At some point, he'd have to go back to the States. His life was there, not that we'd discussed it yet. I kept putting off bringing it up, and I had a feeling he'd been doing the same, both of us living in denial.

His hand cupped the back of my head as he maneuvered me to get a better angle, deepening the kiss the second he did. After a few more moments, I pulled back just enough to break the kiss. He pressed his forehead against mine as we both breathed heavily.

"Your *'stopping for a breather'* didn't quite work to plan, did it?"

Matt laughed raggedly. "It wasn't well thought through, that's for sure."

I glanced in the direction we'd been heading before we'd gotten distracted, unable to see over the edge from where we were stood. "We've probably lost the whale now."

"Maybe. Let's go check," he said, releasing his hold on me and taking my hand before striding toward the railing at the edge of the grass.

As we looked out over the cliff edge, my eyes roamed across the ocean, looking for any splashes that weren't just a break in the water. I shifted so I was looking further right and squealed as I squeezed Matt's hand when I spotted the big dark figure.

"It traveled pretty far," he stated, clearly impressed.

"It's massive, although from up here, it doesn't look that big. But yeah, whales are huge and can probably cover a lot of distance in a short space of time." I smirked. "I don't think that kiss was particularly *short* either."

"I suppose you're right on both accounts." Matt slipped his arm across my shoulders as we both stared out to sea.

It was a moment that felt perfect, but I knew it probably wouldn't last. Life had too many complications for things to be all hearts and flowers forever. But I was going to soak up all the perfect moments I could get so I had the memories to get me through the lonely nights once Matt walked out of my life for good.

CHAPTER EIGHTEEN

MATT

MY MIND WANDERED BACK to our earlier conversation as I watched the whale jump about in the ocean. I didn't know what made Sam ask the question she did, but I was glad she had. As much as I'd been falling deeper for her every minute I spent with her, I needed Sam to know all of me, and that wouldn't have happened if she didn't know those things about my past and who I've loved.

Will was a huge part of my life, and I guess hearing something like that could cause Sam to feel differently about me, although going by that kiss we'd just shared, it didn't change anything.

I cleared my throat and was speaking before I even thought through my words. "Are you okay with what I told you? Like does it bother you that I've been in love with a guy? That I've *been* with a guy?"

Sam shifted under my arm, so I could look into her eyes, which I appreciated because I wasn't certain I could really be sure about what she would say if I couldn't see her emotions while she spoke. "Matt, we all have past lovers, and gender doesn't matter. The fact that they've owned a part of your heart is what matters." I felt a little lighter at the honesty I saw in her eyes. "I'm falling for you, and yes, I worry that you can't feel the same about me. Not because I'm female and Will is male but because I'm concerned he may still own that part of your heart."

I was elated when she said she was falling for me, but the rest of her words were like a sucker punch to the gut. Unsure how to respond, I merely stared at her in silence, which obviously wasn't the response she was hoping for when she turned back to the ocean with a sigh.

"It's okay. I could tell by the way you spoke about him that there was still something there, and I understand. It doesn't change what's between us, and it's not like we can be anything serious, anyway. You're not going to be staying here forever. It's got to end someday and all the better if it's going to be easier for you."

Easier for me? I couldn't believe she thought it would be easier for me. "I may still have some confusion…" The glare she threw my way had me changing my choice of words quickly, "… no, feelings I may still have for Will, but that doesn't make one iota of difference to how I feel about you. I'm falling hard and fast, and it won't be easy for me to leave, not by a long shot. So, don't you dare—"

Sam closed the space between us and crushed her mouth against mine, effectively cutting off my words. Her hands sank into my hair and tugged as she dominated the kiss. I loved it when she took control and got all demanding. I'd noticed it was something she didn't do too often, so I ran with it whenever she felt confident enough to do it.

I groaned into her mouth as her tongue tangled with mine, my hands gripping at her hips to keep myself from grinding my quickly hardening cock against her.

She broke the kiss—far too soon for my liking—and took

some ragged breaths. "We should really take this somewhere else before we get arrested."

A quick glance around, and I found myself agreeing. There was a woman a few feet to our left, hurriedly directing her kids away from us while giving us a dirty look over her shoulder. "Yep. You're right. Let's go home!"

When I said home, I meant Aimee's family's house. It was strange living with Aimee's parents and kids when I didn't even know the woman. I'd offered to pay for a hotel that Sam could share with me, but she'd insisted the Jonas's had welcomed her into their home, and she couldn't throw that back in their face just because I was there. I completely understood this fact, even if it did mean we had to be extra quiet in the bedroom.

BY THE TIME we made it back to the house, we both knew now wasn't the time to carry on from where we'd left things at the beach since it was mid-afternoon, and the house was full of people. So, I suggested we head out for dinner and a movie. Sam agreed that it was a great idea, and she rushed off to 'beautify' herself as she called it. If you asked me, she was talking stupid because she always looked beautiful from what I'd seen, whether she was dressed to the nines or had her face free of makeup and her long dark brown locks scraped back into a messy bun.

I spotted Dan sitting on the sofa, his head bent over an iPad. As I got closer, I could see he was flicking through photos of his mom.

"Hey, little guy," I said as I approached, knowing he was too engrossed in his task to have noticed me.

His head snapped up. "Hi," he offered before quickly

dropping his face back down to the iPad. He wasn't fast enough for me not to notice the wetness in his eyes.

"What are you doing there? Is that your mom?" I asked, knowing full well it was but wanting to toggle him his privacy if he wanted it.

Dan tilted his iPad toward me so I had a clearer view of the pictures and nodded his head. "I was just looking at photos. I wish she were home."

"I bet you do. Does looking at the photos help?"

His shoulders lifted in a shrug. "It doesn't stop me from being sad." His dark brown eyes locked on mine. "Do you miss your mummy?"

A small smile played on my lips at his innocent question. "Sometimes I do. I also miss my bandmates, who are like brothers and sisters to me when we aren't together. Do you know what I do when I want to feel close to them at times when I can't call them?"

He flashed me a smile and nodded eagerly.

"I go outside and take in my surroundings. I feel the ground under my feet and stare at the sky. And then I remind myself that the people I'm missing are on this planet, too. Whether they are in a different time zone or not, they'll also have the ground underneath them and the sky high above them."

A ping came from the iPad, and Dan focused his attention back on it. I couldn't help but also drop my eyes to it to see what had gotten him so excited. It was a text message.

Mummy: *Hey Dan. I'm sorry I'm late with today's photo. I had to wait for the nurse to leave. I hope your mom doesn't kill me for sending you these when she wakes up.*

• • •

THERE WAS another ping and an image popped on the screen of Aimee. She didn't look any different than when we'd seen her a couple of days ago—wires and tubes all over the place. I suddenly wondered whether Dom had really thought his actions through. Should he be sending a kid photographs of his mom in this condition?

Dan laughed and started tapping out a reply on the screen.

DAN: *Thanks Dom. Your braiding is getting better.*

I CHUCKLED as I looked back at the image and the crude braid in Aimee's hair. Dan lifted his eyes to mine, and with a mischievous grin, he started typing more.

DAN: *Matt is laughing at it but he didn't see yesterday's try.*

A REPLY POPPED UP.

MUMMY: *I may have a little sister, but she would've punched me if I ever went near her hair, so I haven't had much practice.*

"THAT'S TRUE. Kat wouldn't let any of us touch her hair when we were kids. Why is Dom braiding your mom's hair?"

"It was messy, and she's always complaining at us if we don't brush our hair. Someone needed to do it for her. And Dom really is getting better."

I shook my head, unable to imagine Dom brushing and

braiding someone's hair. I could tell by the image that he was obviously only doing the bits he could get to around her face, but it was doing a good job of keeping it off her face and away from the wires and tubes, no matter how messy the braid looked.

Heels on the tiled floors sounded behind us, and I turned to find Sam walking toward me. My breath hitched at the sight of her. She looked stunning. Her black jeans were skin-tight and hugging her curves, and the sheer leopard print top she was wearing showed off her lacy bra, not leaving a lot to the imagination. Her hair was hanging loose over her shoulders, and I just wanted to fist my hands in it and pull her lips to mine.

"You look real pretty, Sammy," Dan said, beating me to the compliment.

Sam's face brightened as she winked at Dan. "Thanks, little man."

I stood and walked over to her, twirling a strand of hair around my finger and flicking my eyes between her lips and eyes. "You're so beautiful." I pressed my lips to hers in a soft kiss and smiled as she relaxed into me.

"Ew. That's gross," Dan called out, reminding me he was still in the room with us, and Sam, if her startled jump into my arms was anything to go by.

CHAPTER NINETEEN

SAM

THE IMAGE of Matt staring at me like I was some gorgeous supermodel he wanted to devour was playing in my mind right up until we made it to the bar I'd decided to take him to. Aimee had brought me to Out 'n' Proud once before we left for our trip to America, and the food was delicious. I knew the minute Matt asked where we should go, it was the right place. Although now, standing outside it and thinking back on our earlier conversation on the beach, I was worried about bringing him to a gay bar. What if he thought I had ulterior motives?

Matt wrapped his fingers around mine as we stepped up to the entrance, and the bouncer gave us a nod and waved us in. It was late afternoon, so there wasn't anyone on the stage, but there were plenty of customers eating meals in the booths and tables around the edges of the dance floor.

We chose an empty table in the middle of the room, and a waiter stopped beside us within seconds of our bottoms hitting the seats.

"Hi, welcome to Out 'n' Proud. Have you eaten here before?"

Matt shook his head and said "No," the same time I said "Yes." The waiter flicked his eyes between the two of us, a smile playing on his lips.

"Okay, then. I'll give the newbie the whole spiel." He gave us both a wink and went on, "We have our daily specials on the board over the bar." He pointed them out blindly, but they weren't hard to miss. "And here is the full menu. If you're planning on hanging around for a while, Miss Alotta Bush will be opening the show in an hour. She's hilarious and definitely worth sticking around for."

I flicked my eyes to Matt, giving him the option, but he shrugged.

"I'm happy with whatever as long as I get to call you my date." His wink caused a blush to travel over my cheeks and let my gaze drift away.

"First date?" The waiter asked. "Make sure you share a tiramisu for dessert, it's like a good luck charm for dates turning into long-term relationships," he added without waiting for our answer to his previous question. His eyes traveled to someone over my shoulder, and his face lit up. "Speak of the devils, I was just talking about you two and how you went from first date to a long-term relationship, with just the bite of our tiramisu."

Two guys stopped beside us. The way the smaller, seemingly younger guy was tucked under the bigger guy's arm made the fact that they were a couple unmistakable. "I told you Dane had an unhealthy obsession with you. Are you sure you haven't hooked up before?" the bigger guy said playfully as Dane's cheeks flamed bright enough for us to see in the dimly lit room.

"*Cole!* Stop teasing him," the younger guy elbowed Cole in the side and gave Dane an apologetic smile. "I'm sorry, Dane. Ignore him, he's just…"

Dane shook his head. "It's fine, Scotty. I did have a pretty obvious crush on you when you first got together, so he's not wrong."

Watching the friendly camaraderie between these guys made me wish I could find a group of friends like this. It was currently just Aimee and me, and as much as I adored her, it would be nice to bring people into our fold.

Scotty turned his attention to Matt and me. "Shit, I'm sorry, we didn't mean to hijack your waiter." He turned back to Dane. "Get back to work, you slacker." Scotty frowned and then glanced back at Matt, this time looking at him a little harder.

My heart leaped into my throat as I saw the recognition in his eyes. I didn't want things to change between us, but I knew realistically the minute someone recognized him and word got out, the relaxed time we'd had since landing in Australia would be no more as no matter where we went, he'd most probably get followed by fans and the media.

"Are you who I think you are?" he asked. "You are!"

Matt nodded and offered him his hand. "Matt Dalcin, nice to meet you."

Scotty looked at their joined hands and took a deep breath obviously trying to calm himself down and stop from having a fan-freak-out moment.

"From the band you don't stop listening to?" Cole asked, looking at Matt with wide eyes.

Scotty didn't acknowledge Cole's question but just kept on shaking Matt's hand and staring. Cole took in Scotty's reaction and quickly disentangled him from Matt.

"Come on, Scotty, let's get these two back to their date. It doesn't even look like they've ordered yet," he said as he guided him to an empty table across the other side of the room. When they were only a few steps away, he threw us an apologetic look over his shoulder and mouthed *I'm sorry.*

I turned my attention to Dane, who was giving Matt the

stink eye. "I can't believe I didn't see it. I'm one of your biggest fans." He glanced over his shoulder at Scotty. I followed his gaze with mine and could clearly see the shell-shocked look still plastered on Scotty's face. "Okay, maybe not quite as big as Scotty, but still…"

Matt chuckled. The relaxed smile he was wearing eased my earlier worries about him being recognized, and I felt my lips turn up. "Honestly, you'd be surprised how many people don't recognize me unless I'm with the rest of the band. Saxon is another story… he gets recognized no matter what."

"Does that not make you a little bit jealous?" Dane asked.

"Fuck, no. I like to have privacy now and then. Saxon doesn't know what privacy is, the poor guy, and all because he's the lead singer," Matt said, shaking his head. Anyone could tell he was dead set on that, and I didn't blame him one bit. Not being able to just pop out for a walk or grab something from the shops without being hounded by fans or press must really suck.

"I see your point. Anyway," Dane waved his hand, dismissing the subject. "Have you guys managed to figure out what you want to order, or do you need me to leave you for a minute?"

I flicked my eyes to the painted specials above the bar, and my decision was easy. "Bacon cheeseburger with fries and onion rings for me, please."

Dane scribbled my order down on a piece of paper. "And to drink?"

I noticed a happy hour sign along with the specials, and a quick glance at my watch told me I was good to order a happy hour cocktail. "I'll take whatever vodka cocktail is the most popular."

"One Porn Star Martini coming up."

My eyes widened, but I didn't question it or change my

choice. Maybe a Porn Star Martini was exactly what I needed.

"That sounds promising." I slapped at his arm, and he laughed. "I'll order the same." Matt held the menu out for Dane to take. "Food and drink," he clarified.

"Good choice," Dane offered as he scribbled down the order and picked up my menu. "I'll be back with your drinks in a minute."

I watched him walk over to the register at the bar and key in our orders and couldn't help but wonder what his life was like. Being a writer gave you weird moments like that. Something or someone would spark your interest, and your muse would start dropping little plot bunnies in front of you. I had a feeling there'd be a waiter working in a gay bar coming up in one of my stories very soon.

"What are you thinking about?" Matt asked, his voice drawing my attention away from our waiter and story possibilities.

I shook my head. "Nothing, just a story idea. Nothing that won't save for a rainy day." I offered him a smile and reached across the table for his hand.

"Are you okay?" Matt asked me. My brow furrowed as I tried to work out why he was asking such a thing. "That was our first encounter with a freaked-out Running Hearts' fan. You're still sitting here, so I'm thinking it hasn't scared you away?" His sentence ended on a high note, so it felt like a question rather than a statement, and I treated it as such.

"It'd take more than a fan or two to scare me away." And I meant that. Even an army of crazed fans wouldn't scare me away from Matt. He was the most genuine guy I'd ever met, and I wanted to spend as much time with him as he'd allow.

I knew our time was short since he'd inevitably have to go back to the US soon, and it wasn't like I could follow him around like a lost puppy. Matt had a crazy life filled with gigs and fans, and I was a writer who had just moved to Australia to try life down under. But I was going to make the most of what time we'd have.

CHAPTER TWENTY

MATT

OUR MEAL WAS AMAZING, and Dane was right that the tiramisu was definitely a must-order. He was also right about the show too. Miss Alotta Bush was a fucking hoot, and I laughed from the second she stepped on the stage. Actually, I hadn't really stopped. Sam and I cracked up several times about her on the walk home.

The night air was cool but not too cold that I'd regretted not bringing a jacket with me. My arm rested on Sam's shoulder as we walk, and I tucked her in against my side a little tighter, loving the feel of her curves against my hard lines. I pressed a kiss to the top of her head.

"What was that for?" she asked. I couldn't see the smile on her lips, but I heard it.

"For being here with me. And treating me like a normal person. I don't often get that luxury." I was honest and open. It was something I'd planned to do with Sam knowing whatever we may be building here—be it a long-term and distance relationship or just a friendship—I wanted it to be built on honesty. It was what Sam deserved.

Sam's slender fingers squeezed at my waist. "I wouldn't want to be anywhere else or with anyone but you, Matt."

My cellphone rang, and I pulled it out of my pocket with my spare hand, immediately knowing if I didn't, Sam would only demand I check it in case it was Dom calling about Aimee. Seeing the man in question's name flashing across the screen, I answered immediately.

It was a FaceTime call, and as soon as I caught a glimpse of the battered and bruised blonde on the screen, I held the phone at an angle so Sam could have a clear view of the screen too.

"*OH MY GOD, Aimee!*" Sam called out, stopping in her tracks and raising a hand to her mouth. "I can't believe it's you. I've been so worried."

"I know. I'm sorry. Dom told me how stressed you've been." Aimee moved the camera further away from her, and we could easily see Dom sitting beside her on the small hospital bed. Dom waved, and Sam greeted him.

"Hey, Dom. Aimee, how are you feeling? You sound chirpy enough."

Aimee smiled, but it soon turned to a grimace, making me think those bruises must still be incredibly painful. "I'm sore, but other than that, I feel okay. I just spoke to Mum and the kids. They all seemed pretty excited to hear from me."

"Little Dan has been missing you. They all have... but Dan, especially so. Matt found him scrolling through photos of you not just a few hours ago." I nodded to Sam's explanation and loved feeling her body loosen up beside me. Her worries were drifting away, and that made me happier than I'd imagined.

"Where are you guys? It's dark, and we can hardly see you on the camera."

Sam looked up at me and flashed me a smile before

focusing back on the screen. "We're on a date. We're just walking back from *Out 'n' Proud*."

"What did you think of the place, Matt?"

I didn't really know the woman on the screen before me, but it warmed my heart that she was so open to bringing me into the conversation.

I grinned. "It was amazing, both the food and the entertainment. In fact, we were meant to be going to the movies after our meal but decided to stay there instead."

Sam laughed. "Matt made friends with his number one fan, and we couldn't leave after they joined us on the dance floor." I laughed with her at the memory.

We had tried to leave after a quick dance, but Scotty came over and threw Cole at Sam before grabbing me and forcing me into a friendly dance. He wasn't grabby or inappropriate, so I didn't mind, and it was nice to let my hair down and be a regular guy. Well, close enough to one, anyway. Regular guys didn't have people having fan-freak-out moments, of which Scotty did have a couple of those throughout the night. Dane even joined us on the dance floor once his shift ended, and Sam swapped numbers with them all, so we could arrange to meet up again.

They seemed like a nice group of guys who didn't have a bad bone in their bodies. Some of those rare people that once you found them, you'd be silly not to keep in touch. At least I knew once I left, Sam would have some more friends to have her back. In some of our previous chats, she'd mentioned she and Aimee didn't really have anyone like that.

Aimee yawned, and Dom turned his attention to her and gave her an assessing look. "You're tired," his voice was accusing.

Aimee waved a hand at him. "I'm fine. I've just slept for five days. I think I can manage a few more minutes of conversation."

"You need rest so you can heal."

"Dom's right," Sam agreed, jumping into the conversation. "We'll let you go."

Aimee rolled her eyes but didn't argue. "We'll chat more tomorrow, and you won't be rushing me off the phone even if I'm yawning," she said playfully as she gave Dom a pointed stare.

With a round of goodbyes, we ended the call, and I dropped my cell back into my pocket. Sam was silently crying, so I pulled her against my chest while she got a handle on her emotions.

"I'm so relieved." She sniffed. "I really thought she was never going to wake up. I didn't want to think about never seeing her again, but it was there in the back of my mind every second since I was told she was in a coma."

I stroked my hand up and down her back comfortingly. "It's okay. She's okay. And she'll be coming home soon, I'm sure."

I felt Sam's head move against my chest in a nod and pressed a kiss to the top of her head. After another minute or two's silence, she took a deep yet shaky breath and stepped back out of my arms. "Let's go home. I have a feeling they'll be celebrating, and I'd love to join them."

And we did just that.

By the time we arrived at the house, Sarah and Spencer were well on their way to drunk, and the boys were all on a sugar high. After the phone call, Sarah had sent Spencer to the local liquor store, where he seemingly cleared them out of champagne and chocolates. There were two empty bottles on the kitchen counter and another opened and half-drunk bottle in the refrigerator alongside four other full and chilled bottles. We had enough bubbles to keep us partying well into the night.

And that was exactly what we did.

CHAPTER TWENTY-ONE

SAM

IT HAD BEEN ALMOST two weeks since Aimee woke up, and we were all waiting impatiently for her to return home. I paced up and down the waiting area outside the arrivals gate, my eyes flicking to the door every ten seconds waiting for it to open. Nobody had come out as yet, and I knew even when people did start exiting, Aimee wouldn't be one of the first.

Matt threw an arm out and grabbed my bicep as I passed him before pulling me to a stop before him. "You're making me dizzy."

I slid my arms around his waist and looked up at him, a small smile lifting my lips at the corners. He was a good eight inches taller than me, and when he held me like this, I felt protected and safe. I loved it.

Dan shot by us with a squeal of excitement, and I knew before even turning around that Aimee had just walked through the door. I hung back with Matt as the kids greeted their mom. Matt released me and pulled Dom into a man hug. I decided Aimee's family had hogged her enough, and I needed a hug from my bestie.

I threw my arms around her neck and squeezed her tight.

Aimee laughed. "I can't breathe, Sammy."

"I don't care. I'm never letting go," I said with a smile, only half-joking. I'd missed her a lot even though we'd chatted most days since she has woken and went back to texting pretty much all day like we had when I lived in Germany and her in Aussieland. I guess I'd gotten used to having her around in the flesh, and the rest just wasn't good enough anymore.

"You can't get freaky with Matt if you don't let me go."

That got me to let her go. I held her at arm's length as I snapped my eyes to hers and gave her a guilty stare.

"I knew it!" she announced, the smile on her face dropping for a second. "I kind of feel insulted that you didn't tell me. You better give me all the details later."

I nodded, and she turned toward Dom, who Matt was quietly chatting with. Aimee and I usually told each other everything, but while she was recovering, I didn't feel like I should tell her about what had been going on between Matt and me. I felt like she needed to focus on getting herself better and passing whatever tests the doctors needed to run to allow her to fly home. And really, I didn't know what was going on between Matt and me. Well, I knew how I felt, but I had no idea how it was going to work when Matt headed back to the US or even if there'd be anything to make work then. Maybe what we have now is just a bit of fun like a holiday fling.

A holiday fling that I'd never get over.

Aimee noticed we were attracting attention, so we left before even introducing Dom to Aimee's family. Once we got to the cars—Aimee's and her dad's—I offered her the keys. "Do you want to drive?"

I might have my own car that sat on her driveway, but I wasn't quite used to driving on the wrong side of the road yet and preferred not to drive if I didn't have to. So when she took the keys off me with a smile, I sighed with relief.

WE WEREN'T HOME long before we decided to have a family movie session. I smiled as I watched how close Aimee and Dom were. Matt told me Dom was feeling things for Aimee, but I was certain it was guilt over having knocked her unconscious. However, watching how he looked at her almost reverently, I could see that Matt was right. And the feeling was clearly mutual by the way she returned his looks. I was looking forward to having a good gossip with Aimee, so I could find out how things had gotten so serious with them so soon.

It inspired me, seeing them make the most of what they had and seemly not care about what obstacles the future might throw at them. So, I pushed all my worries away and decided then and there while settling down to watch the movie that Dan had picked, I'd take a leaf out of their books and make the most of every second I had.

I didn't pay much attention to the figures on the screen. Instead, I curled up against Matt's side on the L-shaped sofa and concentrated on his beating heart under my fingertips.

"Are you even watching this?" Matt whispered against my ear, a smirk discernible in his voice.

I shook my head in answer, not wanting to disturb the movie, and turned to offer him a smile. He linked his fingers in mine resting on his chest and stroked at my wrist with his thumb.

CHAPTER TWENTY-TWO

MATT

THE KIDS somehow managed to talk their way out of school and into a trip to the zoo with the four of us. They quizzed Aimee the whole way from the cars until we'd paid and actually entered the place, clearly waiting for someone to jump out and tell them it was a prank, and they were really going to school. I could only imagine they'd been on the same journey to the zoo, waiting for Aimee to turn the car around and head for their schools. Sam and I had had a kid-free ride, but the way Chris was hanging off Sam's every word made me think our trip home might be different.

I stepped up alongside Dom and asked him something that had been playing on my mind for a few days. "How did the impromptu gig come about?"

The gig in question was recorded by a fan just a day or so before Dom and Aimee left the US. The video went viral. It's all over the internet, and the media was going crazy over the songs they sung, ones we'd written before we got a record deal and the label didn't want us to sing.

I saw him shrug out of the corner of my eye. "It was crazy.

We got recognized, and the band who were performing called us up. They didn't really give us a choice."

"But the songs?" I asked, wanting him to clarify the main thing that was bugging me.

"We were in a honky-tonk. If we didn't sing some country tunes, we'd probably have been booed off the stage." We both laughed at his comment because it was likely true. "Besides, I needed a bass player, and I didn't think Will would know our regular stuff."

My heart leaped at hearing his name. That was another thing I wanted to ask Dom about. Why was Will there? Why was he with the band onstage? But I wasn't going to come out and ask about him because nobody knew there had been anything more than a friendship between the two of us back in the day. Nobody even questioned it when we stopped talking after Will walked away from the band, even while he kept in touch with the other guys.

"Did he?" I asked, curious about whether he'd followed our music.

Dom chuckled. "No. He actually thanked me afterward for playing the old music because he wouldn't have been able to play any of our current stuff."

"I haven't seen him in years. How's he doing?" I knew exactly how he was. Anytime Kat or Dom mentioned him, I paid attention, but I was always happy to find out new stuff.

"He's good. He didn't want to get onstage but was buzzing when we finished. So I'm certain he enjoyed every second up there."

"Dom! Look at this croc," Dan called out from up ahead. Dan had seemingly taken a shine to Dom, and seeing how much he cared for Aimee, it was wonderful to watch. Dom offered me an apologetic smile before leaving our conversation unfinished and heading off to look at whatever Dan was so excited about. Intrigued, I followed behind.

———

SAM LOOKED AT ME, curiosity clear in her lifted brow and piercing stare. "What's on your mind?" I frowned, and she went on as I closed the bedroom door behind me. "You've been quiet all night. I'm worried."

"You heard when Dom got the call from Gary, our manager?" Dom had taken the call after we arrived back from the zoo. Apparently, with everyone going insane for our new sound due to the viral video, the record company wanted us to focus on that for our next album, which we were apparently writing here in Australia. Not only that, but Gary was sending the rest of the band out here, which now included Will and Alberto, even though they originally chose to walk away from the band.

Sam nodded. "Yeah. It's exciting, isn't it?"

I stepped over to her desk and started picking up random knick-knacks—a Yoda Pop Vinyl and a piece of jewelry that looked like a time turner from *Harry Potter*. I spun it between my fingers as I spoke, not daring to look at Sam's face. I didn't want to see any hurt my words might cause.

"I'm worried about seeing Will again. I don't want it to change anything between us, but I'm worried him being here will."

I heard the bedding shift and felt her hand brush against the small of my back before her lips pressed against my shoulder blade. "I don't know what we have here. I know what I'd like it to be, but I'm also aware that there are plenty of obstacles ahead of us if it's going to go that way, and yes, Will might be one. Worrying about what might happen is a waste of energy that could be spent doing something else." She kissed a trail across my shoulders and stepped around my front before looking up at me with her chocolate-brown eyes.

I grinned down at her. "I like the sound of this *something else* you speak of."

"I thought you might." She reached up on her tiptoes and pressed a kiss to my lips, the kiss soon turning to something more passionate.

CHAPTER TWENTY-THREE

SAM

I'D KNOWN what Matt was worried about before I'd even asked him. It was obvious the moment Dom had told him Will was coming, and he'd gone unusually quiet and distant. I'd be lying if I didn't admit it did concern me, but like Aimee ass always reminding me, *what's meant to be will be.* Nothing I would do could change that, so I was going to make the most of what I had with Matt while I could. If Will came and destroyed it all, then so be it. I'd be left with a broken heart, but I would have put my all into it.

I pulled back from the kiss and stripped out of my clothes as Matt's hungry eyes followed my every movement. "You're so beautiful."

He trailed a finger down my neck and over my breast, giving my nipple enough attention to make it pebble. My breath came in short pants, and I arched my back, hoping he'd give them more attention.

"You're pretty damn beautiful yourself, but you have way too many clothes on right now."

Matt chuckled. "I've only got my boxer shorts on."

I slipped my fingers into the waistband of his boxers. "It's covering some very important bits." I slowly slid them down his legs and dropped to my knees as they got lower. He stepped out of them when they were low enough, and I ran my hands up his thighs before sliding them over his ass cheeks, squeezing them. His cock was hard and bobbed enticingly when I was at eye level with it. I wanted to taste him, so I leaned forward and slid my lips around it.

It was salty and tangy with precum, but it wasn't unpleasant. In fact, it excited me knowing I'd turned him on this much. Matt groaned when he was fully engulfed, and I slid my mouth off and urged him to lay down on the bed.

Once he was laid back and in the position I wanted him to be in, I crawled up between his legs and licked my way down his cock. I wrapped my hand around his shaft and sucked on one of his balls before moving to the other, making him shift beneath me on the bed and groan with encouragement, my hand moving up and down in a rhythm he was clearly enjoying.

"Ugh, fuck, you're good at that."

Knowing he'd just had a shower, I let my tongue dip lower and tease over his hole. He'd made it clear he was bi, so I was pretty sure he wouldn't be opposed to a bit of anal play. Besides, I knew straight couples who enjoyed anal play.

Matt's breath hitched, and a moan escaped as I pressed my tongue harder against the pulsating hole and breaching the rim a fraction. Once I felt like he was slippery enough with my saliva, I pressed my thumb against the damp rim and teased it slightly.

"Is this okay?" I asked, wanting to give him the chance to say no if it wasn't what he wanted.

"Fuck, yeah. I haven't had anyone's mouth there in… too long. Girls don't usually do that."

I pressed my thumb inside, and it went without much force, telling me he was relaxed and comfortable enough for more, but I licked the rim and up his taint as I stroked my thumb in and out just to be sure. "Throw me the lube out of the drawer on my side of the bed."

He shifted slightly on the bed, and I heard the drawer open and close before something hit the mattress beside his leg. I hastily smothered two fingers in the cold liquid before pressing them against his puckered hole.

"Please," he whimpered, moving his hips to try and get my fingers where he wanted them.

I licked my way up his cock as I slowly pressed my fingers inside him, pausing once they were fully seated to give him time to get used to the intrusion.

He squirmed. "Sammy, I need you to move those beautiful fingers of yours."

"Patience, Matt. You need to learn some patience if you want this to be good," I said with a laugh.

"Oh, this is already more than good." His voice caught as I slid my fingers out, giving him what he'd asked for.

Once my fingertips were breaching the rim, I opened my mouth, and with my other hand wrapped around his shaft, I guided it into my warm, wet mouth at the same torturously slow pace as I slid my fingers back inside him.

"Fuck. Fuck. Fuck." His words were chant-like, and I had a feeling he didn't even realize he was speaking them out loud.

After a few more thrusts, my mouth and fingers working in unison, I picked up my pace, and I knew I was pegging the magic spot inside because Matt was groaning and bucking beneath me with every thrust.

"Sam, I love what you're doing and how your fingers feel, but I want to fuck you. Right now."

I pulled my mouth off his cock but kept my fingers going, making sure to hit his G-spot as I bit at my lip, wondering whether I should suggest what I was thinking. I didn't want it to ruin the moment—his moment.

"Sam… now. Please."

Deciding to risk it, I blurted out what was on the tip of my tongue. "I have a butt plug. Do you want to…?"

"Oh god, yes. Is it in the… drawer?" His sentence was breathy, and I knew he was close.

Wanting him to come inside me, I pulled my fingers out and pressed a kiss to his hip. "Yes. Grab a condom, too."

He twisted his body, and I knew he was actually looking in the drawer this time, not just blindly reaching inside. "You have a butt plug? Do you like anal play too, then?"

I nodded when his eyes locked onto mine as he waited for my answer.

He smiled. "Good, I like giving it, too." He focused back on the drawer, pulling out the butt plug and condom. His hand flicked around in the drawer for another second before he pulled out my vibrator. "I'd love to fuck you with this while I take your ass one day if you'd be up for that."

Need started to pool in my stomach, and my pussy throbbed at the idea. "Yeah, I'd like that. A lot." I couldn't believe I was being so open about my sexual fantasies with him, but having just had my tongue where it was, I guessed we couldn't really get any more intimate.

Matt put the vibrator back in the drawer and passed the butt plug to my hand. "Do you want the honors?"

I grinned. "I do." I lubed up the toy and pressed it against his ass. "Ready?"

"More than ready. Hurry up so I can fuck you already."

I did as he asked while he rolled on the condom, only pausing once to groan as he got used to the plug. He laid back and crooked a finger at me in a come-here gesture. I crawled up his body and straddled his hips, making sure to grind my pussy against the hard shaft lying against his stomach. We both moaned, and I crushed my mouth against his once I could reach it.

Matt flipped us over, and I was suddenly on my back looking up into his hazel eyes, his pupils blown out with arousal. "You're amazing. Do you know that?"

"Maybe you should show me."

His fingers brushed against my pussy between us, and I let my legs drop apart, trying to give him all the room he needed. "You're so fucking wet. You really do like anal play, even dishing it out."

I nodded, unable to speak as his finger slipped inside me, thrusting once, twice, before another finger joined it. After another couple of thrusts, his fingers left me, and I whimpered at the loss.

"It's all right, baby, I'm gonna fill you up with something else." Matt pressed a kiss to my lips.

I felt the tip of his cock brush against my opening and wrapped my legs around his thigh, trying to get him to enter me quicker.

"Patience, Sammy." The teasing was clear in his voice as he used my earlier words against me, but I didn't care because he sank into me in one quick, deep thrust, and it felt amazing.

CHAPTER TWENTY-FOUR

MATT

SAM'S BREATHS were coming in a deep and steady rhythm which told me she was already asleep. I couldn't quite manage the same as my mind was ticking over with thoughts about what she'd just done for me and how intimate we'd become from the one sexual encounter. No girl had ever played with my ass before. I'll admit, for a split second, I worried Sam was only doing it because we'd spoken about Will, and maybe she thought if she did things he'd do, I wouldn't want him. As she carried on without hesitation and seemingly working with experience, I realized she was doing something she wanted to do. Maybe even something she craved and needed too.

It shouldn't surprise me because every day I spent with her, I felt she was more and more perfect, like she was made for me.

It was only an hour later that I heard my phone beep, and I reached over to silence it before it woke up Sam. Seeing an email from Gary, I clicked the notification to open it and couldn't believe my eyes. It was an itinerary for Al, Kat, and Will's flights. They'd be here in two days. The guy worked quickly, I'd give him that.

If I'd read it earlier in the night, I would've been terrified, but after what Sam and I had just done, I felt like I could get through it. I could face my first love and maybe manage to mend a friendship while I was at it.

Feeling more at peace than I had in a long time, I placed my phone back on the side table after clicking it to silent and pulled Sam tighter into my arms. I was soon drifting off to sleep with the feel of her heart beating beneath my palm.

———

THE TWO DAYS passed by quicker than I'd imagined it would, and I found myself staring at the glass doors we'd been waiting for Aimee and Dom to walk out of less than a week earlier. The doors finally opened, and as my eyes fell on Will —an older-looking Will than I remembered—my heart skipped a beat as I was taken back to a long-forgotten day.

I LOOKED ACROSS THE ROOM, and my eyes found him immediately. It had been two days since we kissed, and I couldn't stop thinking about him. His gentle kisses mixed with the rough stubble brushing against my lips were surprisingly sexy.

Will's attention was on the woman before him, and the fact that he seemed interested in her had jealousy raging through me. I needed to get a grip. He was one of my best buddies, and no one knew I even liked guys. Hell, I hadn't known I liked guys until that kiss.

As though he could feel me watching him, his eyes flicked across to mine. I didn't know what he saw, but whatever it was, it had his brows almost hitting his hairline. Leaning forward, he gave the woman what looked like an apologetic smile as he said something I couldn't decipher.

Within seconds, he was striding up to me with a primal look on his face. "We need to leave," he commanded, stepping around me and walking to the exit, ignoring anyone who tried to stop him on the way.

I followed him without question. I didn't know what was going on between us, but whatever it was and going by that look I'd seen on his face, I wasn't the only one feeling it.

Once out of the ballroom where the event had been happening, Will didn't stop. Instead, he pressed the button on the elevator, and we stood in silence waiting for the doors to open. His shoulders were ramrod straight, and his tension was almost palpable.

When the doors opened, there were a couple of girls in there who let out an excited whisper. We stood back and let them pass as they exited. Thankfully, they weren't confident enough to stop us and ask for photos or autographs, or maybe they could sense the tension around us. It most certainly felt palpable to me, and I couldn't wait to get somewhere more private, so I could find out what it would lead to.

I WAS SUDDENLY FLOODED with feelings, the same feelings I'd had all those years ago when we were kids messing around. We messed around a hell of a lot back then until Will had had enough of my hiding us behind closed doors and left the band.

The good feelings were suddenly washed away by hatred of myself. I had a beautiful woman on my arm, one I'd fallen for in the last few weeks, and here I was still in love with a guy I hadn't seen for years. How could I be in love with two people at once?

CHAPTER TWENTY-FIVE

WILL

THE FLIGHT WAS AS LONG as I'd imagine and so much more dreadful than I'd thought. The three of us had been seated together, which was great because we managed to play cards and chat about old times when we'd found ourselves bored of binge-watching whatever we'd found that caught our interest on the airline's entertainment system. The worst thing about the entire time was that we had a poor single mom behind us with a baby who screamed nonstop and a slightly older kid—maybe five years old—who kicked my chair the majority of the way. I felt so sorry for her and hoped to god she had someone waiting for her on the other side of those arrival doors to take the kids off her hands, so she could enjoy some well-deserved peace and quiet.

I watched the bedraggled woman tug along the tired and cranky kid as the baby strapped to her chest in some strange carrier contraption slept soundlessly, looking like a sweet little angel. Those of us who were seated near her knew differently, though. She hurried past me and reached out for a large suitcase, missing it because the boy wouldn't let go of her hand long enough to let her grab it. As the suitcase was within my reach, I pulled it off the conveyor belt, and after righting it on its wheels, I pushed it in her direction.

"I believe this is yours?"

She offered me a grateful smile, her shoulders drooping in relief. "Thank you so much." She glanced at her son before giving me a sheepish look. "I'm so sorry about the chair kicking. I did keep telling him, but…"

"It's okay, it was a long flight for me, and I'm an adult. I can't imagine how bored the little guy was." I reached out and ruffled his hair, getting a giggle from him.

"Thank you." She sounded more appreciative than I'd have thought, but as the guy who sat beside her and her kids passed and glared at her, I realized why. It made me wonder if he'd been giving her looks like that during the flight or, even worse, making nasty comments to her. You could tell the poor woman felt bad enough as it was when she really couldn't have changed the situation. For whatever reason, she needed to be on that flight and had every right to be on it just as he had. I hated people like that guy. If I'd have heard him, I'd have given him my two cents then and there on the flight.

"Do you have someone out there waiting for you?" I asked, nodding to the gate, my eyes widened as I belatedly realized how that could've sounded like I was coming onto her. "I mean to help you get your bags in the car or whatever transport you're using?"

She laughed, clearly amused by my embarrassment, and nodded. "Yes, my husband. We've emigrated, and he came out first with his job, and they helped him get set up in a house."

"That's amazing. Congratulations." I caught sight of Al and Kat both giving me irritated looks, both of them having their suitcases in hand while mine was most probably going around on its fourth turn since I'd been too distracted to bother looking for it. I gave them a nod before turning my attention back to the woman before me. "It was lovely meeting you and your little ones. I wish you all the best for this new chapter in your life."

Seeing my bag coming up quickly and not wanting to miss it, I dashed off for it, not giving her a chance to thank me again. Since she'd said it to me several times already, I could hazard a guess that she'd have ended the conversation on it again.

"That brat did nothing but kick your seat for ten hours straight, and you just ruffled his hair like he was a sweet little angel. Are you nuts, or do you just have a seriously bad memory?" Alberto asked as he weighed me up like he'd be able to see the answer to his question on me somehow.

I laughed. "That poor mother had a worse flight than either of us. I was just being nice to her."

"Aww," Kat crooned as she hooked her arm into mine and cuddled up to me. "You're such a sweet guy."

Al pretended to gag. "I didn't travel all the way to Australia to watch my sister flirt with my bandmate." He frowned. "Jesus, I never thought I'd be saying that again. My bandmate…"

The air around us seemed to turn serious, and I nodded. "I know the feeling. I never thought I'd be doing this. Not after I passed it up the first time."

Kat leaned back, just enough to weigh me up without actually letting me go. "Are you ever going to tell us the real reason why you walked away back then? Because I don't think anyone believed whatever lie it was you spun."

I sighed. I wanted to tell them. Hell, I left because I didn't want to hide, and then I hid anyway because I never told the truth about why I walked away from the band. I shook my head and shrugged at the same time. "I don't know. Maybe one day."

I always hoped that *one day* things would change.

Maybe *one day* Matt would see that we could be ourselves without the whole world hating us.

And *one day* pigs might fly.

CHAPTER TWENTY-SIX

SAM

I FELT Matt stiffen beside me as a tall blond guy walked through the opened doors, and then I recognized the woman hanging off his arm as Kat, Dom's sister and the drummer of Running Hearts.

Alberto was just behind them, frowning over his shoulder at someone or something. Being an author, I couldn't help but be curious about that little mystery, but I probably never would find out.

The handsome blond smirked as his eyes landed on Aimee and Dom, who had taken a moment to share a kiss. "How come you two are always sucking face when I'm around?"

"They're always sucking face," Matt stated, his voice shaking slightly with nerves.

Will's gaze turned to Matt. Leaving Kat, he changed direction and came to a stop before us. He was even better-looking close up. His blue eyes sparkled like sapphires, and his biceps were undeniably magnificent, bulging beneath his t-shirt with even the slightest of movements.

"It's been a long time since we saw each other, Will," Matt

offered, sounding nervous and unsure. "This is Sam… Samantha." He flicked his gaze to me questioningly, obviously not knowing how I wanted to be introduced.

Will offered me a smile and held his hand toward me. "It's lovely to meet you, Samantha."

"You, too, Will. I've heard a lot about you." His eyes flicked to Matt beside me, and I worried I'd said the wrong thing. Would the others be suspicious about the fact that Matt had been talking about Will to me, or would it be expected?

"Matt. It's good to see you again." They shook hands and had an awkward man-hug moment that both didn't seem comfortable doing. When they broke apart, I slipped my hand into Matt's and gave it a gentle squeeze of reassurance.

Will sighed. "It has been a long time." He turned away, seemingly ending the conversation, but I heard his whispered, "too long," wondering whether he meant for it to be heard or not.

The longing in his voice made it clear I needed to find a way to get these two somewhere private so they could talk, and soon, because they both seemed to have a lot on their minds when it came to each other. I wanted them to at least clear the air and try to fix their friendship. Otherwise, I worried they'd never be able to work together. And that was exactly why they were all here. The band's future relied on the five of them meshing and working together like a well-oiled machine.

Will gave Dom a similar hug to Matt, only he looked much more relaxed this time. "And, fair warning, we don't suck face half as much as these two," I heard Dom state as he hooked a thumb over his shoulder, gesturing toward Matt and me.

I gave him wide eyes and gasped, dropping my jaw to make my mouth an 'O' in mock offense.

"You know it's true," Aimee said as she offered me a quirked brow.

I huffed. "Fine. Whatever." My lips quirked as I started to lose the ability to suppress my laugh.

Kat pushed her way past Will and jumped at Dom. "We're actually having a holiday in Australia. Can you believe it?"

Dom laughed as he wrapped his sister in his arms. "*I* was having a holiday until Gary called and told me he was sending you guys to join me so we could *work*."

"Oh hush," she said as she shoved at his chest playfully, making him take a step back. "Stop ruining my good vibes. Gary isn't here to make sure we work twenty-four seven like he probably he intended, so I'm sure we can at least make this into a working holiday."

I liked that idea. When Aimee and I went on our trip to America, we'd planned to write as much as we could and, to be honest, we kind of failed there. So, it would be nice to get back to some writing and marketing for our businesses because our sales were most certainly suffering from the lack of authoring we'd been doing as of late.

"Hey," I tugged at Matt's arm, pulling him out of a trance he seemed to have fallen into somewhere along the way. "Are you okay?"

He gulped in a deep breath and flicked his eyes from Will, who he'd been transfixed by, to me. "Yeah, sorry… I just—"

I placed my finger over his lips, cutting him off. "You don't need to explain. I understand." And I did. He'd already told me about their past, therefore I was expecting some kind of reaction, so him freezing like that wasn't unexpected. The corners of his mouth curled up into a small smile beneath my finger, and I pulled it away, satisfied he wasn't going to try to explain more. I turned to look back at the others, so I could go and greet them, but Matt caught my bicep, turning me back to him and pressed an unhurried kiss to my lips.

"Thank you," he said against my lips before straightening and letting me finally turn toward the others.

Alberto was chatting to Dom as Will and Aimee hugged each other like old friends. I belatedly realized Aimee had time to get to know everyone after she'd woken from her coma. She'd clearly made connections with these guys. It made me somewhat jealous that I'd not really had that chance. The only person I'd been able to get to know was Matt, and as much as I was grateful for that, it would've been nice to spend time with the people who obviously meant the world to him — his family — even if they were his chosen family.

Kat's beautiful face and her blonde pixie cut blocked my view of the others as she threw her arms around me and drew me into a full-body hug. "Hey, girl! If that kiss was anything to go by, Matt finally made a move. I'm so glad because once the paparazzi get a shot of you guys, they'll know the stupid rumors of me and him were never true. Just because we aren't related and are the opposite sex, it doesn't mean we have to be dating."

I looked at her wide-eyed while she ranted about people and their assumptions. Matt's arm slipped over my shoulder, and he tugged me against his side. "Way to go, Kat. If you actually want the paps to see us together, I'd suggest you don't scare her away before they find us."

I looked up at him to catch him mid-eye-roll and let out a laugh as Kat thumped his arm.

"Shut up and hug me. I missed you."

Matt gave her a one-armed hug, not releasing me even though I squirmed to try to get free. "It's been what... two weeks? If that."

Alberto walked over and gave Matt a high-five before offering me a shy wave. Al had kept to himself while I was in America. Possibly avoiding the crazy woman that was me, and I didn't really blame him, since most of that time I was either biting Dom's head off for knocking Aimee out in the first place or stressing over whether she was going to wake before our return flights to Australia—or even at all.

CHAPTER TWENTY-SEVEN

WILL

SETTING my eyes upon the person who I'd once thought was the love of my life was harder than I'd imagined. But when his hazel gaze locked onto mine, I knew, at that moment, he was still the love of my life. The pang in my chest made that perfectly clear.

Over the years since I'd walked away, we'd managed to stay apart. I connected with the others when they came in for tattoos or on nights out when Matt had other plans and wouldn't be there. I never really imagined I'd still feel so strongly about him after all this time.

The beautiful brunette beside him seemed to hint at knowing about our past. I didn't know if that was a good or bad thing, but there was nothing I could do to change what knowledge she may or may not have about what transpired between us, so I brushed my uneasiness aside.

"Let's get out of here before we garner the attention we don't want. It'd be nice to have a few days of peace before the vultures swoop in," Dom offered, reminding me once again that taking this step back into the band meant I was stepping into the limelight and throwing away the privacy I'd enjoyed over the last few years. If I were honest, I'd admit the thought terrified me, but the chance to see what I'd been missing all these years outweighed that terror, even if only a little.

When we arrived at the two cars parked side by side, there was no discussion about who would jump in with who. Kat and Al just automatically gravitated toward the one that Dom was in, which wasn't surprising when I thought about it since they were siblings, after all. So that left me to jump in the deep end and join Matt and Sam because squeezing in the back seat of the other car would've been uncomfortable and left everyone else with questions about why I'd avoided traveling with Matt.

After placing my suitcase into the trunk of the car, I slid silently into the back seat. The first five minutes of the trip were tense, and I kept running over things I could say in my mind but decided not to say them out loud. Or more honestly, just not being brave enough to, but I didn't need to worry because Samantha broke the silence.

"Okay. I can't take the silence anymore. You guys need to talk…" She flicked her eyes to meet mine in the mirror before going back to the road. "You can talk shit or get the important stuff off your chest while you have the privacy of this car because I'm not sure what privacy you'll get back home, where we'll be packed in like sardines."

I wasn't sure what Matt had told her about our past, and I didn't know how comfortable either of us would be being open and honest with her listening in.

As if she could read my mind, she spoke again. "Matt has been open with me to a point about your past relationship." She reached across the center console and took Matt's hand in hers, clearly offering comfort. I couldn't help but wish I had someone to provide me with comfort. Her gaze met mine again in the mirror. "I can put my earbuds in and crank the music if that would make you more comfortable."

It was Matt's turn to offer Sam a warm, grateful smile.

I shook my head. "That won't be necessary. You and Matt are together, and that means you have every right to hear our conversation." I didn't want to come between them, and if we spoke away from Samantha, it would forever hang over their relationship. She'd wonder what was said and whether what he told her about it was the truth.

Matt turned in his seat to be able to look at me while still wearing his belt. "I've had this conversation in my head a million times, and yet now we're here, I have no idea what to say."

I chuckled. "I was pretty much thinking the same thing." I felt the tension leave my body, and I released a relaxing breath. "I'm sorry I walked away like I did without giving you a chance to change things—"

Matt cut me off with a resounding, "*No.*" He was shaking his head and looked at me with pleading eyes. "Don't think like that. I was never going to be brave enough to give you what you wanted. I wish things were different. I still do. There isn't a day that goes by that I don't think about what could've been, but it is what it is, and I want you to know that I'm sorry."

My heart constricted in my chest at his words, knowing he still thought about us like that just as I did. He offered me a weary smile, his deep-set eyes locked on mine. I'd always thought of him as handsome, but he was even more so now, having grown into his features and losing the softness of a boy from his face and having them replaced with the harder edges of a man.

I smiled back and let myself think of a future where we could work together. I may not have known where things were going to go or how we'd move on from here, but what I did know was that I wanted to close this vast void between us and mend both our broken hearts in the process.

CHAPTER TWENTY-EIGHT

MATT

EVEN THOUGH WILL and I didn't really have a deep and meaningful chat, it was enough to clear the air and break the ice all at once. The remainder of the ride home was filled with general chit-chat between the three of us.

We'd barely made it into the Jonas's house before the sibling rivalry started, and I wasn't talking about Aimee's kids.

"I'm not sharing with him again," Kat whined, clearly referring to her younger years. "Why can't the guys share?"

"Look, I'll share. Hell, I'll sleep on the floor if I have to. It's not like it'll be the first time," Will offered. My lips turned up into a smirk remembering one of the times Will—and I—slept on the floor. I wasn't certain Will was even referring to that night, but it was one of my favorite memories.

WILL ROLLED US OVER, demanding he be on top, but I felt nothing underneath me except air as we rolled off the bed. He twisted at the last minute and landed with a thud, his back on the floor and letting out an 'oomph.'

I couldn't help but let out a chuckle.

"I save your back, and you laugh. Well, that's the last time I'll be chivalrous." Will's words seemed annoyed, but his voice was full of amusement.

I buried my face against his chest as I tried not to laugh anymore, and I said a muffled, "I'm sorry."

He shifted his hips, and our hard cocks rubbed against each other between us, reminding me what we had in the middle of us and causing all thoughts of laughing to disappear.

I groaned. "Do that again." I shifted on top of him, causing the delectable friction again.

"It seems like you've got that covered yourself," Will offered as he dug his fingers into my hips, helping me slide against him.

That gave me an idea of what we were missing. "Hands... yes." I slipped my hand between us and half our cocks together—my hand didn't go fully around the two cocks, and Will released a hip and let his hand join mine between us. The extra pressure was just what I needed, and as I slid against him, I felt my orgasm getting closer. The grunts he was making told me he was close too. I upped my pace, and my climax rushed over me, making me spill my seed over both our stomachs. As if I'd caused a chain reaction, there were more warm and wet fluids joining mine as Will came too.

Releasing our cocks, I pulled my hand free from between us and collapsed on top of Will, knowing Will loved it when I did that. The first time we had sex, I made an effort to collapse to the side, but Will just pulled me right back on top of him, telling me he loved the feel of my body against him, all sated and relaxed.

He pressed his lips against my forehead. "I love you."

My heart skipped a beat. We'd been having sex for a few weeks now, and even though my feelings had grown for him, I'd never let myself hope he was feeling anything similar, but now he'd uttered the words, I was elated. I lifted my head enough to catch his bright blue gaze. "I love you, too."

He offered me a warm smile as he stroked his hand up and down *my back. "I'd suggest we move back to bed, but I don't think any of my muscles will cooperate just yet."*

"Same," I said as I lay my face back against his chest, soaking in the feel of his hard muscles beneath me and the beat of his heart against my ear. "Maybe we could just sleep here," I suggested, not wanting to move and break whatever spell we were under.

He lifted his arm and tugged the covers off the bed. "Good idea," he agreed.

I knew by morning we'd both regret not moving, mainly because of the sticky mess between us, but at that moment, I couldn't make myself care about that. I was naked and wrapped in the love of my life's arms. There was nowhere else I'd rather be.

"NOBODY WILL BE SLEEPING on the floor. We have enough beds. Unfortunately, we just don't have enough rooms for everyone to have their own," Sarah said, her voice was laced with an apology.

"Ma'am, I'm Will. Thank you so much for letting us into your lovely home."

Sarah visibly swooned at Will but took his offered hand in hers and gave him a shy, "You're welcome."

"Okay. It's decided then. Al and Will can share Dan's room. Kat, you'll be in the motorhome outside." Aimee's voice was commanding, she was clearly using her mom voice, and the three parties in question nodded along in agreement, seemingly not brave enough to disagree. I couldn't exactly blame them.

Dan appeared, seemingly from out of nowhere and stopped in front of Will. "Hey, I'm Dan. Want me to show you where my room is?"

Will gave Dan an amused grin. "Sure. That'll be great." He flicked a look to Al, who was still standing in the entryway. "Al, come on. We have a guide showing us to his room."

"Awesome. I hope we have a space theme," Al responded as he rushed forward to follow.

"Sorry. I grew out of space stuff. I'm into dragons now."

"Dragons are way cooler than space. Look at this…" I heard Will offer and knew he'd be pulling his sleeve up to show Dan the dragon tattoo he has flying over his bicep and shoulder. That was his first tattoo, and I remembered it well. He'd probably gotten a lot more over the years we'd been apart which I'd be interested to see. Tattoos always told a story about a person.

"I'm grabbing a drink. Does anyone else want a beer?" Sam offered from beside me.

Dropping a kiss to the top of her head, I agreed. "That's a great idea." She gave me a warm smile as I let go of her hand and watched her walk toward the kitchen, a sexy sway to her hips making me want to drag her off to our private room.

CHAPTER TWENTY-NINE

SAM

THE FIRST DAY and night with everyone in the house went by quickly. Spencer hosted an amazing welcoming barbecue, and we all hung out listening to music and playing pool. We even had a water bomb fight with the kids in the heat of the afternoon. I'd been living in Australia for a few months now, but I still struggled with the heat. Aimee had been here for years and still complained, so I wasn't holding any hope of ever getting accustomed to it.

I was making my elixir of life—also known as coffee—when Sarah and Spencer joined me in the kitchen. Will stumbled out of the bedroom he was sharing with Al, rubbing a hand over his face.

"Oh, Samantha, could I get one of those, too?" he asked, eyeing the coffee pod in my hand.

"Of course, what intensity do you like?" I asked, knowing people could be picky about their coffee. Aimee and I both liked the lower numbers best, and her parents wouldn't touch anything under ten, so we had a whole range of pods from five right up to thirteen.

"I'll take anything as long as it has caffeine in it." He rubbed his fingertips over his eyes.

I laughed at the movement, even though I wondered why he didn't sleep longer if he was still so tired. It wasn't like anyone had made big plans for today, having all suffered from jet lag after our arrival here. "Maybe you need a double shot."

Will grimaced and shook his head. "No, I'll be bouncing off the walls if I do that. Y'all would have to tie me down."

I bit my lip as I turned toward the coffee machine and went about making his drink, all the while not being able to erase the image of him tied to a chair, naked. I knew that wasn't what he meant, but my dirty mind had jumped straight to the gutter with his words.

It only took a couple of minutes for the machine to do its thing, and I breathed in the scent of coffee as it filled the air.

"Oh my god, I need one of those," Aimee stated as she made her way to join the rest of us in the kitchen.

"Well, you'll have to wait your turn because there's a queue," Spencer stated from where he'd been leaning against the counter, his arms draped over Sarah's shoulders, her back against his front as they watched Will's and my exchange.

"I'm so sorry. I should've waited," Will apologized.

Sarah shook her head and playfully elbowed her husband in the stomach. "Look what you did." She focused back on Will. "Guests always get served first, Will. We wouldn't have it any other way."

I handed him his mug and went about making my own, adding more milk to mine once the machine had finished doing its thing because I didn't like it super strong. I stepped aside and let Spencer have the machine. I glanced at Will looking out the French doors that led from the house to the backyard.

"The sun won't be too hot right now if you want to go sit outside while you wait for the coffee to kick in. It's like our little morning gathering place." I opened the door and stepped out, a smile ghosting my lips as I heard him follow me.

We both sat, and Will yawned as he took in the scenery.

"You know, you could've just stayed in bed," I suggested as I sipped at my cup. "Even if you'd heard us moving around, I have a feeling your body wouldn't have been against you going back over."

"I want to avoid jet lag, so sticking to my normal sleep pattern in this time zone is my plan."

I nodded, figuring that made sense, and I stepped out from under the shade. Closing my eyes, I lifted my face to the sky and basked in the warmth of the sun's rays on my skin, breathing in the clean, fresh air as I listened to the birds twittering away in the trees. Australia may have a hell of a lot of creatures that want to kill you, but nature was loud and beautiful here, and it definitely made the risk of those deadly things worth it.

The wicker chair creaked, and I opened my eyes to see Will had taken the seat with the best view. The house was higher than the neighboring houses behind, so we could see the mountains in the distance right over their roofs. "It's beautiful, isn't it?"

Will nodded and flicked his eyes my way as I sat in the chair next to his. "It's not the only thing that is."

My breath caught, and I couldn't help but wonder if he was talking about me. It sure felt like that, especially with the steady and certain look he was giving me.

"Morning, guys," Aimee called out, breaking the tense moment as she joined us. To tell the truth, I was grateful for it because I wasn't sure how to respond to Will. She bent down and pressed her head against mine in a friendly hug before pressing a quick kiss to Will's cheek.

"Morning, sweetie, is your man still sleeping, too?" I asked with a chuckle. Matt and Dom were both such sleepyheads, but then again, Aimee and I loved our sleep too, so maybe we had both found our perfect matches. My heart sank at the thought. I didn't know how either of us were going to keep the guys we'd found, whether or not they were perfect for us. Our lives were worlds apart from the guys.

"He's in the shower. I gave him a happy wake-up call." She threw me a wink, making me laugh. It was good to see her being so open and enjoying that intimate side of a relationship for once. We'd been friends for a long time, and I knew how bad things were with her ex-husband and the way he made her feel about sex.

Will groaned and hung his head, rubbing a hand over his face. "I didn't need to hear that."

Sarah and Spencer joined us, Alberto following close behind, all of them with cups in hand, filling up the remaining seats on the outside lounge chairs.

Sarah looked at Aimee as she placed her coffee cup on the low table where all the chairs were placed around. "Me and your dad have been talking, and since the kids are going to their dad's this weekend, we're going to head out in the motorhome." Aimee opened her mouth, but Sarah held up a hand to stop her and carried on talking, "I know Kat has just gotten settled in there, but she can have our room while we're away. I just think it will give you young ones time to bond. That's what that fancy manager man said the band needed, right?"

"You don't have to do that, Sarah. We won't have trouble meshing together as a band. We've been one before, and we all grew up together, so we'll be perfectly fine and up to Gary's standards of bonded in no time," Dom said as he stepped up to Aimee's chair and hoisted her out before taking the seat himself and pulling her down into his lap. Aimee's giggle was infectious, and I found myself smiling along with her.

"Oh, we aren't going out of our way. We haven't had a weekend away in forever. It's definitely needed. As long as Kat is okay with moving rooms for the weekend, that is," Sarah stated.

Dom weighed Sarah up for a minute, obviously assessing whether she was being completely honest or not. To be fair, I was doing the same, and she seemed genuinely excited at the prospect of a trip away. He nodded. "I'm sure Kat won't mind at all."

"What won't I mind?" Kat asked as she joined us in the yard. "Ooh, and where can I get myself one of those?" She pointed to a mug, and I stood, deciding it was most definitely time to wake up Matt.

"Take my seat. I'm going to kick Matt out of bed, and I'll make you a coffee on the way past." Kat offered me a grateful smile as we traded places.

The coffee machine was already whirring when I stepped into the house, and since the kids weren't coffee drinkers, I knew it was Matt before I rounded the corner. I slipped my hands around his waist, enjoying the feel of his abs contracting under my fingertips as I pressed a kiss against his bare back.

"Morning, beautiful." He turned in my arms, and I pressed a kiss against his chest before lifting my face to his.

"Good morning, handsome."

Matt ducked his head and touched his lips to mine. He shifted back, but I didn't let him get far. I tangled my fingers into the hair on his nape and crushed my mouth against his, probing at the seam of his lips with my tongue. He opened to me instantly, groaning into my mouth while cupping my face with one hand and allowing the other to roam down my body. I loved it when he went all out like this, losing himself in the moment with me. I'd never before felt as sexy as I did in moments like this.

CHAPTER THIRTY

MATT

Sarah and Spencer left after lunch. It took three of us to direct Spencer out with the motorhome. It was a tight fit, and, at one point, I thought he was going to knock the rain gutter off the roof.

Aimee joined us all in the yard after seeing the kids out to their dad. She looked a little sad, and I couldn't help myself watching as Dom wrapped her in his arms and whispered something in her ear before pressing his lips against her forehead. They were a cute couple, and I was thrilled he'd found someone who made him as happy as Aimee obviously did.

"Annnd... we have fire!" a beaming Sam called out from the fire burning nicer than it had been when Will and Al had been trying to light it ten minutes ago.

We ate, played pool, and chatted about old times for hours. It felt like the old days, except with the fantastic additions of the beautiful brunette who sat in my lap and the blonde curled into Dom's side.

Aimee straightened, and her face lit up with excitement. "Let's go clubbing!"

"Oh, I like that idea," Kat agreed, practically bouncing in her seat.

Dom looked between the two girls. "Well, by the looks of you two, even if we say no, you're going anyway. So, I'm in."

"Ugh, I'm comfy. I don't think I can face it," Sam said, and I felt her sentiment. I didn't want to go to a busy club and spend the night looking over my shoulder, wondering which drunken person around us was going to recognize the Running Hearts' members and announce our whereabouts all over social media.

"Yeah, count me out. If we all go, we'd most probably wake up in the morning with the press camped outside."

"Shit, I didn't think of that." Aimee leaned back against Dom. "Maybe we shouldn't go." She sounded so deflated, I wanted to take back my words.

"I haven't been part of the band for ages, so nobody will recognize me," Al offered.

"You were in the video that went viral. It was the whole reason Gary sent you guys here. Matt's right, we can't go," Aimee stated, clearly seeing my point.

Dom ran a hand through his hair and stood, tugging Aimee up afterward. "We'll be fine, especially if the whole band isn't there."

"I'll stay here, too," Will added.

"See, they won't recognize the original band with Matt missing, and with Will not there, they won't flashback to the show from the honky-tonk," Dom offered as he pulled Aimee's bottom lip from between her teeth, where she'd been worrying it.

"Ooh goodie, now that's decided, let's go get dolled up." Kat grabbed Aimee's hand and pulled her toward the house. Aimee gave Dom a worried glance over her shoulder.

Dom waved her off with a grin. "Go. I promise it'll be fine."

———

TWENTY MINUTES LATER, they were shouting their goodbyes and walking out the front door.

Sam sighed and relaxed against me. "I thought Aimee was going to try to talk me into going with them, then you brought up the paparazzi, and I thought they'd stay. Aimee could do with a night out dancing. I'm glad they went."

"Me, too," I admitted.

Will leaned forward in his seat and placed his hands on his knees as though he was going to stand. "Maybe I should've gone, too. I'll head to bed, and then at least you guys can have some alone time."

Sam practically leaped off my lap. "No," she cried as she sat in another chair. "I like that it's just the three of us. You mean a lot to Matt, and he means a lot to me, so I'd love to get to know you more, Will." Even in the firelight, I could see the flush creep over her face.

Will offered a nervous nod. In a way, I felt apprehensive too. I wanted them to get along, but I also felt like there was a lot for Will and me to mend, and I wasn't at all sure where to start. Luckily, Sam had a plan for that too.

"I know… let's play *Truth or Dare*." She flicked her eyes at us, and when they landed on the empty beer bottles on the table, so she jumped up. "I'm gonna grab us all some drinks first. I'll be right back." She disappeared into the house, leaving Will and me watching after her.

"She's something else," Will stated, bringing a smile to my face. We always had similar tastes in women and even shared one or two back in the day. That was before we ever touched each other, though. Once we'd discovered we were sexually attracted to each other, the idea of having a girl with us seemed to fall to the back of our minds.

Now, though, part of me was more than interested in

seeing what the three of us could manage together, and by Will's comment, maybe he was thinking the same thing.

I raised a brow, and I locked eyes with him. "She sure is. Are you interested?"

Will waved me off. "You guys seem happy, and I'm here to try and make this whole band thing work. I think me trying to rip your girl from your arms would be counterproductive for that."

I laughed because he was totally right, but I also hadn't exactly meant that. Unfortunately, I didn't have time to correct him before Sam joined us again, carrying six beer bottles with her. "Have you got enough beers there? Or are you already seeing double?"

"Ha ha," she said with a roll of her eyes. "I figured if I brought six, I wouldn't have to go back to the fridge so soon." She held one out to Will and he took the bottle with a shrug. "She has a good point."

The game started out pretty tame, the dares being *'do your party trick'* or *'do your best dance move.'* It was after the third trip to the fridge when things started to get a little wild.

When it was Sam's turn for a truth, she licked her lips and flicked her eyes between the two of us. The uncertainty that crossed her face had me a little anxious. "I can't stop imagining you two kissing… I want to know if it's as sexy as I imagine."

Will's eyes practically bugged out of his head at her suggestion. I sunk my teeth into my bottom lip to try to suppress a laugh.

"I'm sorry. I know it was wrong of me even to bring that up. You guys are trying to fix your relationship, and here I am bringing up things that would no doubt muddle up your feelings even more." She cleared her throat and nudged me with her toes. "Quick, give me a dare."

"No. You said your truth. It's my turn." I stared at her, wishing she was able to read my mind. "Give *me* a dare."

I needed it to come from her to know she was absolutely certain that was what she wanted because suggesting something and meaning it were two completely different things.

Sam stared at me for a long time before she gave me what I wanted. "I dare you to kiss Will."

I stood and stepped over to Will, stopping in front of his chair. "This one is kind of a two-man dare, so what do you say? You up for it?"

Will took in a sharp breath and nodded. "I... yeah. Okay." He stood, and I pounced, crushing my mouth against his before he had a chance to change his mind. He opened his mouth on a gasp, and I took the opportunity to slide my tongue inside and stroke at his.

"Holy shit. You two are hotter than I imagined. So much hotter." Sam's words had Will and me breaking apart.

I smirked at her. "You ain't seen nothing yet." Knowing if she really did like that—and it sure sounded like she did— she'd enjoy seeing us do other stuff together even more.

Sam hung her head in her hands and groaned. "*Matt,*" she whined. "Did you really have to put more images in my head?"

Will and I both laughed as I tugged her into my arms. "Now, kiss me before we give you your dare," I ordered. She complied, immediately wrapping her hands around my neck and nibbling at my lips before I opened to her. She was so fucking sexy, and just the idea of her liking what she saw between Will and me had me hard as a rock in my pants.

I adjusted myself before sitting down again and feeling Will's gaze on me. I met it with mine. Something passed between us. It was like we were back in the old days. He raised a questioning brow at me, and I smirked in answer. His lips raised at the corners, and he turned to face Sam.

"It's your turn for a dare now, Samantha."

She swallowed nervously but nodded in agreement.

"I dare you to tell us exactly what more you imagined us doing to each other and then take us both to bed so we can all play out your fantasy." My heart started beating rapidly in my chest as I watched Sam with bated breath, waiting for her response.

"I… I don't think I can."

Will's smile dropped off his face and was replaced with a serious look. "Okay. Then let's end this now. I'm going to head to bed. I'll see you both in the morning." My heart took a dive too, but I was more disappointed on Will's behalf, knowing he wouldn't be getting any love or attention tonight after thinking he maybe would.

"*Wait!*" Sam called out. "That's not what I meant. I may have read and written gay romance… hell, I've even watched gay porn, but I don't think that would be the same as seeing two guys who have genuine feelings for each other together. I can't tell you guys what to do because part of the fantasy is you guys doing what you want to each other."

"Do you really mean that?" I asked as I grabbed her hand in mine.

She nodded. "I do."

I chewed on my lip as I rolled ideas around in my head. I wanted them both more than anything, but I also needed to know they were both on the same page as me. "If you guys really want to do this, you need to know that it will change everything from here on out." I flicked my eyes between the two of them, trying to read their thoughts. "It won't be just one night. And, Sam, it won't just be me and Will. All three of us need to be equal in this."

"We can't expect Will would want me like that." Sam gave Will a shy look. "I'd be okay if he just wanted to share you."

Will shook his head. "Samantha, that won't be a problem.

I more than like you like that. I'd offer to show you how much now, but I think you probably need a few minutes to get your head around this, and it would be better to be somewhere a little more comfortable before we get into that kind of thing."

A look of worry suddenly crossed Sam's face as she gave us both wide eyes. "Shit. I need to freshen up. I'll meet you guys in the bedroom." She strode off toward the house, and I laughed. That was when I'd discovered she meant she wanted to have a shower, shave her legs, and primp herself in whatever way girls did before being intimate with a guy.

"Feel free to get started without me," she called over her shoulder, her words making my dick twitch with anticipation. My eyes fell on Will, who looked just as eager as I felt.

I suddenly felt like tonight was going to be so much more interesting than I'd originally thought it would be. And I couldn't wait to get started.

CHAPTER THIRTY-ONE

SAM

HAVING JUST HAD A SHOWER, I headed back to my room wearing a light robe with just my underwear beneath. My heart beat erratically as my nerves started to get the better of me. With all the flirting and teasing by the fire tonight—the more alcohol we consumed, the more outrageous we got—it was more than obvious where things were heading between the three of us. It was something I wanted more than I ever could've imagined.

At first, I'd felt guilty for being attracted to Will when I was with Matt. But the chemistry between the three of us was undeniable. So once Matt assured me he was more than okay with me being interested in Will too, I decided to follow my gut, or heart, or whatever it was, and just dive into the moment. After all, I'd already promised myself to do that a few days ago when watching Dom and Aimee together.

I stepped into the room with my eyes on the floor, only lifting them when I'd closed the door behind me. My breath hitched as my gaze fell on a naked and turned-on Matt, who was laid out on the bed with his hands tied to the headboard with one of my scarves. The sight had the heat growing within me, and I let out a needy whimper.

"You okay, baby?" Matt asked, his dark hair flopped over his forehead that was shining with sweat.

"If you've changed your mind and want me to leave, just say the word, and I will go now," Will offered. My head spun to the side, and my eyes landed on the handsome blond I hadn't even noticed in the room before he spoke. His blue eyes were full of sincerity, and I knew he meant what he'd said.

"I haven't. I want this. Matt. You. The three of us," I said, not looking away, even when I felt my face flush with the embarrassment of how honest I was being and how vulnerable it made me feel. *What if they didn't want me here as much as they wanted each other?* I wanted him to see the truth in my words.

He nodded, but it was Matt who spoke, "Take off the robe, Sammy. Show Will that sexy body of yours."

I untied the sash and slipped the silky material over my shoulders, letting it drop to the floor and pool at my bare feet.

My eyes flicked from Matt's heated hazel gaze to Will's. He was biting his lip and giving me an appraising look, making it more than obvious he wasn't just in the room for Matt.

The look he was giving me caused my breath to come in short pants, and I licked my lips at the thought of what he might be thinking he'd like to do to me. It made me feel sexier than I'd ever felt.

"You like him looking at you, don't you, Sammy?"

Unable to think straight enough to string a sentence together, I nodded as I gazed back at Matt, who was shifting on the bed, most likely trying to get some friction on his hard cock. He groaned in pleasure, and I looked at him closer. There was something black peeking out from between his ass cheeks, and as I realized what it was, moisture pooled in my panties.

"Do you want him to touch you?"

Again, I couldn't get my mouth to form words, so I nodded as I let my gaze drift to Will, hoping he could see the pleading in my eyes.

"Will, you heard her. Tell me if she's wet for us."

Will swallowed and strode toward me with long, sure strides. Stopping beside me, he reached out and slid his fingertips over my side and down to my hip, stopping as they brushed the waistband of my panties. "Is this okay, Samantha?" I'd always hated my full name, but the way he said it, so sensually, sent my heart racing and my clit throbbing.

I offered him a smile and nod. It seemed like that was all I was doing, but I couldn't manage to do anything more.

A finger dipped under the lace, and the others joined in. He never dropped his gaze from mine, making the moment feel intimate and so arousing. His forefinger brushed over my clit, and I widened my stance as it kept going on its descent through my folds. I moaned as more of his hand brushed over my clit, and two of his digits sank into my entrance.

"Fuck, she's so wet, Matty," he said as he removed his fingers. I whimpered at the loss and watched him hungrily as he sucked my juices from his fingers and moaned around them. "She tastes good, too." He turned from looking over his shoulder at Matt to back to me as I bit painfully at my bottom lip. "Do you want a taste, Samantha?"

"Yes," I whispered breathlessly.

He took my chin in his fingers and tilted my head up as he bent down and brushed his lips against mine, gently, almost experimentally. When I opened for him, his tongue swept in my mouth, and he deepened the kiss. I could taste myself on him, and it wasn't unpleasant. He pulled away, and I tried to chase him for more.

He chuckled. "There'll be more of those, but let's join Matt. I have a feeling he'll be needing some attention now."

"Fuck, yes. I need to taste you, Sammy. Come here."

His pleading tone had me leaving Will standing by the door and climbing onto the bed. I leaned over to press my lips to his, but he shook his head and gave me a wicked look.

"No, Sammy. I want to taste your other lips. Sit on my face." His words had me trembling in anticipation as I removed my lace panties. Once I had my lower half bared, I didn't wait around. Worry about being practically naked with two guys in the room flickered through my mind, but I felt safe and sexy with their eyes on me as I straddled Matt and moved up his body to position myself where he'd instructed. I reached up and gripped the headboard as his tongue flicked over my clit, and my eyes closed as I basked in the sensation.

The sound of material shifting caught my attention, and I looked over my shoulder at Will stepping out of his shorts and boxers. His t-shirt was no longer on his shoulders, and his muscular tattoo-covered body was deliciously naked. I had a sudden urge to take a close look at each one of his tattoos, but his long, thick cock was what had my full attention once my eyes landed on it, and that was what I wanted to explore right at that moment. There'd be plenty of time for his tattoos later.

CHAPTER THIRTY-TWO

WILL

SAM'S deep brown orbs flitted over my body almost errati-cally. It was like she didn't know what she wanted to look at first. Her eyes finally settled on my cock, and the attention she gave it caused it to twitch. I wrapped my palm around it and leisurely stroked up its length while watching her ride Matt's face, his fingers pressed into her hips guiding her movements.

Fuck, they looked hot together.

Sam beckoned me with a crooked finger. "Come join us, Will." Her head fell back, and she released a moan. "Mmm… Matt, right there. Yes."

Releasing my cock, I walked over to the bed, my heart racing the entire way. When I'd agreed to give this joining-the-band thing a go, I'd thought Matt and I could put the past behind us and get some closure. I'd never in my wildest dreams imagined we'd be starting over and with an extra person involved too. I stopped beside the bed, and Matt's eyes locked on mine from between Sam's thighs.

She offered me a smile as she picked up her pace on Matt's mouth. "I think Matt's cock deserves some attention.

Do you think you're up for that?" I was usually the dominant one in the bedroom, but with me joining them, I suddenly felt the urge to hold that part of me back—at least for tonight, anyway—needing Sam to be the instigator to be sure I was welcomed into the fold. I didn't lie when I'd said I would leave if she changed her mind.

I crawled onto the bed and kneeled between Matt's thighs, spreading them wide enough for me to see the butt plug between his cheeks. He groaned at the movement, and his cock jumped against his stomach, a trail of precum on his tanned flesh.

I wrapped my hand around his shaft and lowered my head so that I could take it into my mouth. It had been too long since I'd tasted him, and I was suddenly desperate to rectify that.

I hummed around his cock as it slid against my tongue and into my throat. Matt's hips bucked beneath me, and he hit the back of my throat, causing my eyes to water. I didn't care. I'd craved this for so long, and now that I had it, I wasn't stopping for anything.

"Fuck," Sam cried out, and I lifted my eyes from Matt's abs to find her eyes trained on me as she looked over her shoulder. Her movements became erratic, and I knew she was chasing her orgasm.

I couldn't see Matt's mouth from this angle, but when she screamed with ecstasy, it was clear he'd hit the right spot. She snapped her back around and rested it against the headboard as Matt supported her with his hands still on her hips.

I sucked my way up Matt's cock and swirled my tongue around the head. "Shit, Will. Have you been practicing?"

I pulled my mouth off his cock with a pop and chuckled. He was right to question me. The last time we'd tried this, we were both inexperienced and had no idea what we were doing. I had since had a fair bit of practice, but I was pretty certain, knowing Matt, he wouldn't want me to really answer that question.

I licked my way back down his cock and sucked one of his balls into my mouth before giving the other one the same treatment. I heard movement above me, but I was too engrossed in what I was doing that I didn't want to turn my attention away for even a second. I licked over his taint and swirled my tongue around his rim and the butt plug there.

"Fuuuck," he called out breathlessly.

"You guys are so fucking hot. Mmm…" Sam's moan had my gaze snapping to her propped against the pillows beside Matt, her legs parted and her fingers playing over her clit.

"*Shit.*" My cock jumped at the sight, and I gripped it with my hand, squeezing it to try to ease the sudden need I had.

"I need you to fuck me, Will," Matt said, sounding more than a little desperate.

Sam's fingers traveled lower, and one digit dipped inside her pussy. I thought we all needed to fuck, and quickly.

"Are you ready for that, Matt? You said it had been a while. I don't want to hurt you."

Sam's eyes locked on mine, and I watched as a blush spread across her cheeks. "We've played. He'll be able to take you."

As much as her certain statement had my curiosity piqued, the need to fuck won out over any questioning. I pulled out the plug and watched his greedy hole pulsate.

I sucked my fingers into my mouth, making sure they were nice and wet from my saliva before sliding two of them into his hole. They went without any resistance, and I was confident that he was ready for my dick. I pumped my fingers once, twice, before pulling them out.

Matt whimpered at the loss. "Someone untie me. I want us all to be connected."

Sam removed her fingers from her pussy and squeezed

her thighs together as she turned to take care of the scarf around Matt's wrists.

"Do you have any lube?" I asked, hoping they weren't going to say no. I hadn't thought to bring any with me, not expecting to have sex at all, let alone with a guy.

Matt.

I still couldn't believe I was here in this situation with Matt.

My Matt.

CHAPTER THIRTY-THREE

MATT

ONCE THE SCARF WAS GONE, I lowered my hands and twisted them around before rubbing at my wrists to get the blood flowing freely again. It wasn't like Will had tied the scarf too tight, but my hands had been in that position above my head for quite some time, and my fingers were tingling with numbness.

Eager to get back to where we were going, I ignored the pins and needles and reached into the drawer beside my head. I pulled out two condoms and the tube of lube we had in there and threw the lube to Will. He caught it easily and held out his hand for a condom.

"Let me," Sam said as she snagged them out of my hand. She brushed a kiss against my mouth, and with a quick probe at the seam with my tongue, I deepened it when she opened to me. She pulled away, too quick for my liking, but I let her go without a fight, well aware I wasn't the only person who wanted in on the action.

I propped myself up on my elbows as I watched her move down the bed, coming to a stop beside Will, who was sitting back on his heels between my thighs. His tongue flicked across his bottom lip, and Sam leaned forward, clearly taking that as an invitation. She groaned as their mouths came together, the sound causing my already hard cock to harden even more.

Leaning on just one elbow, I wrapped a hand around my cock and started stroking myself as I happily watched them make out. They looked good together.

When Will arrived, and I realized I still had feelings for him, I was more than ready to ignore that and focus on Sam and my feelings for her. However, when they both made it obvious they were attracted to each other too, the idea of the three of us together felt right. I didn't know how it was going to work in the long run, but right now, this was perfect. It would be something I'd remember and treasure for the rest of my life.

Sam broke the kiss, and Will chased her to press another closed-mouth kiss to her lips. "You're good with that mouth of yours."

"You don't know nothing yet," I teased, knowing exactly how good she was with her mouth.

He dropped his head back and groaned miserably. "Ugh. Don't tease me. We don't have time for that right now."

"We've got all night," Sam offered with a shrug.

"Nuh-uh." Will shook his head. "Fucking. We are fucking as soon as we're suited up. So hand over that condom, Samantha." He held out his hand and wiggled his fingers in a give-me gesture.

"C-can I do it?" she asked, her voice sounding unsure.

Will dropped his hands to his sides and nodded. "Of course."

Sam pressed a quick kiss to his lips and went about tearing the foil wrapper open. I watched as Will held his breath while Sam reached out for him.

Sam turned her body, and I got a clear view of Will's

condom-covered cock. My balls tingled, and my cock twitched at the thought of where his cock would be in a few minutes. Sam's hand brushed against mine, and I lifted my eyes to hers. She offered me a smile and showed me the other condom in her hand, already out of its wrapper.

"Suit me up, baby, because I'm so ready to fuck you," I stated, offering her what I hoped was a sexy grin.

Looking from Sam to Will, my heart swelled in my chest. I was so elated to be here sharing this moment with them.

The two people I'd grown to love most in the world.

CHAPTER THIRTY-FOUR

SAM

I CLOSED my eyes as Matt finally sunk his glorious dick into me. Watching Will blow Matt turned me on more than I could've imagined. I couldn't help but ease the need with my fingers, and when Will looked up and cursed after seeing what I was doing… Let's just say I've never been wetter.

I could see Will over his shoulder, and as Matt pressed a kiss to my collarbone, Will pressed one against Matt's neck, his eyes locked to mine the whole time. It felt so intimate, and in a way, it felt like he was kissing me.

"You okay?"

Matt's question tore my attention from Will, my eyes leaving bright blue orbs and meeting a hazel set shining with arousal.

"*Yes,*" I offered, my voice coming out breathier than I'd expected.

Matt pulled back and thrust back inside me, causing me to moan in pleasure. He suddenly stiffened above me, his eyes narrowed and lips pursed in wariness. Knowing that meant Will must have been making a move, I decided Matt needed a distraction to relax so as not to end up being hurt. I lifted my elbows until my mouth pressed against his and licked against the seam of his lips. I felt the tension leave his body as he opened to me and took over the kiss, plunging his tongue into my mouth. I gave as good as I got, swallowing his moan as Will slid inside him.

Warmth radiated through me as I heard both Will and Matt release deep sighs of contentment, the sound making me more than happy. All three of us were soon moving in unison, coming together as if this was always how it was meant to be —taking and giving at the same time. It was beautiful, and my body tingled with pleasure as my orgasm got closer and closer.

Matt's movements picked up the pace, and Will's thrusts had him slamming into me harder and harder with each one.

"*Oh, yes,*" I cried out as my climax soared over me, and my pussy clenched around Matt's cock.

"*Fuck!*" Will called out as Matt grunted and collapsed between us.

Tears streamed down Matt's cheeks, and if it weren't for the small smile playing at his lips, I'd worry he'd been hurt. Instead, his elation told me he needed us both. He needed the softness of a woman and the hardness of a man, and by the look in Will's eyes, he understood that as much as I did.

Will rolled to the side, taking Matt's weight with him so neither of them were crushing me. I turned to follow them, pressing a kiss on Matt's forehead as he laid flat on his back, his arm covering his eyes beside me, breathing heavy, with Will on his other side. I was suddenly glad I'd bought a larger bed and given up floor space for it. There'd be nothing worse than there not being enough room for the three of us to recover side by side like this.

Will got up, and I watched his muscles jump as he pulled his boxers on and headed for the bedroom door. I caught his eye as he passed and frowned. "I'll be back. I'm just getting you both something to clean up with," he offered me, a wicked smile plastered on his face as he slipped out the door.

My clit throbbed, and I squeezed my thighs together to ease the fresh wave of need rolling over me.

"I can't believe I did that." Matt's voice was small and insecure, so much so that it washed all thoughts of sexy things away, and I shifted in the bed so I was resting on my folded arms over his chest. I dropped a kiss on his pec just above his heart before lifting my gaze to his face.

"What? Had some amazing sex?" I asked, keeping my voice light and playful, hoping to put him at ease and keep him talking. I didn't want him to bury whatever thoughts and emotions were going through him at that moment because that wouldn't be good for any of us. For things between the three of us to work, we had to be honest and open.

Matt lifted his arm off his face and wiped at the wetness under his eyes. "No, I mean crying like a baby. I feel like an idiot."

The door clicked shut, and I glanced over my shoulder to find Will back in the room, a washcloth in each hand.

"You're not the first person I've had cry on me after sex. I should've warned you it's a regular occurrence for me, I'm just that good." Will grinned, looking self-assured, and I bit my lip as I waited with bated breath to see how Matt was going to react to that comment. I felt like it could've gone either way.

The bed started to shake, and I looked back at Matt and found him chuckling.

"You always were a cocky bastard," he admonished with a shake of his head, his eyes sparkling with humor.

A giggle broke free from my mouth, and I buried my face against Matt's chest as I let my amusement loose.

A wet cloth slapped against my back as another brushed my elbow as it landed on Matt's stomach. "I was going to take care of you both, but since you find the idea of me giving someone great sex so amusing, I don't think either of you deserve it."

The bed dipped, and I felt Will take hold of the washcloth on my back and slide it down over my behind, stopping at the crease of my thigh. He tapped my inner thighs with a finger. "Spread your legs, Samantha."

There he went with his sexy way of saying my name, causing my breath to hitch and my clit to throb with a fresh wave of need.

Maybe they'd be up for another round?

CHAPTER THIRTY-FIVE

MATT - THREE WEEKS LATER

MY PHONE STARTED BUZZING, and I grumbled sleepily about the stupid goddamn alarm that had pulled me from an awesome dream.

"Fuck!" Was it really six in the morning already? After that first night together, Will had been sneaking into our room every night after Al fell asleep, and we'd set the alarm extra early so he could go back before anyone woke up.

"Ugh… someone turn the stupid thing off," Sam mumbled, annoyance clear in her voice. It may have been a couple of weeks, but Sam still hadn't come around to the early wake-up calls. I'd learned early on that Sam wasn't a morning person, and it was not smart to wake her unless I had a cup of coffee in hand for her.

I shifted in the bed, rolling over to grab my phone, and like most days these last few weeks, I found myself pressed up against a hard muscular body. My arms brushed over Will's abs as I reached over him for my phone, and memories of all the nights the three of us had spent together here—and all the wicked things we'd done—flooded my mind.

"Morning." Will gave me a smirk that told me he had a

good idea about what I was thinking. Obviously, it was written all over my face.

I hit the stop button and pulled my arm back, letting it slowly trail over his abs, taking my time to feel every ridge. It reminded me of the morning after the first night.

I ROLLED OVER, and instead of finding empty space, I found a hard muscular body curled against me, my fingers brushing his abs. I'd quickly moved back. I didn't know why. I wanted to touch him more than anything, but I didn't know what the fuck was going on with the three of us and where either of their heads were at. Hell, I didn't even know where my head was at.

"Hey," I said, distracted, as I turned over to check on Sam.

"Stop stressing, Matt. I can practically hear your internal freak-out."

I laughed nervously, and that sound alone showed them both how right Sam was.

Sam moved to her side, bringing us face to face. She pressed a closed-mouth kiss to my lips and pulled back. "Roll onto your back. There's someone else who wants in on the morning kisses."

Doing as I was told, I moved so I was flat on my back. Sam molded herself against my side, leaning an arm over my abs and rising her chin on my pec as she looked across my body at Will watching us both with an unreadable glint in his eyes.

"Come here, handsome."

Will followed her order, turning so he mirrored her position against my other side and didn't stop moving until his mouth was pressed against hers in a chaste kiss.

Sam made it clear she wasn't in the mood for chaste as she probed at the seam of his lips. He gave in, opening for her, and I got a front-row view. My dick grew harder with every sound of pleasure the pair of them made, and by the time Sam finally decided she was happy to break the kiss, I had a raging boner.

"Good morning, Will," Sam offered, her eyes locked on Will's.

"It certainly is, Samantha." Will's lips were turned up at the corners in amusement. Sam shivered, and I watched his amusement turn into a satisfied grin. My lips twitched too. She got turned on by him calling her Samantha. I didn't blame her as it was the sexiest I'd ever heard anyone say her name.

"MATT," Dom's voice called out from the other side of the bedroom door, pulling me out of my memories as he tapped his knuckles against the wood. "Do you know where Will is? He asked me to go over some songs with him today, and I can't find him."

I looked at Will with wide eyes, not knowing what to do. Everyone could see mine and Will's friendship had returned to what it once was, and the three of us got along like a house on fire, but we'd kept what was going on between us in private—just that—private.

Will opened his mouth, and without thought, I quickly slapped my hand over it before he could get a word out.

"Last night, he said he was going to get up early for a run. Something about wanting to clear his head." As soon as the words left my mouth, I knew it was the wrong thing to do. Will's shoulders slumped in defeat as he lifted himself off me, and my hand slipped away from his mouth.

I flicked my eyes to Sam who was looking at me with what I could only describe as disappointment. I felt like such a dick, but this moment made it clear to me that this— between the three of us—couldn't work long term, not when I couldn't even bring myself to tell my best friend about it. When Dom knocked on that door, a fear I'd never felt before overtook me. I was terrified that he'd open the door and see us all together.

The silence pressed down on me as Will dressed, and I couldn't take it any longer. "Will, let me explain."

Will shook his head. "You don't need to. I should've known nothing had changed even after all these years. You're still in the closet, and you always will be. I was a fool even to hope it would be any other way."

Sam slipped off the bed and grabbed his arm, halting his exit. "Wait, Will, don't leave." Her voice wobbled with emotion.

Will cupped her face with his palm. "We'll talk later, I promise," he offered, his voice full of affection. "But right now, I need to clear my head, so I'm going to actually go for that run."

They both stared at each other for a moment, and something passed between them as I watched. Maybe Will shouldn't be the one running. They both deserved happiness, and I was the one stopping them from having it in the way they wanted because I was scared.

I was running scared.

CHAPTER THIRTY-SIX

WILL

IT KILLED me to leave the room and those two amazing people behind, but I knew if I stayed, I'd be the dirty little secret kept behind closed doors. I didn't want to live like that. I couldn't live like that when the band first got together, and nothing had changed for me.

I didn't sneak through the house since I wasn't ashamed of who I was or what had transpired in Samantha's bedroom, but lucky for Matt, I didn't bump into anyone on my way to the room I'd been sleeping in with Al. Al was out like a light like he was at this time every morning, so I quickly threw my running gear on and went for a run.

The sun and fresh air didn't do much good to calm my anger, but it did help me realize I was doing the right thing. I wasn't angry at Matt, not really. I'd known his feelings about his bisexuality and his need to keep it locked away. I was angrier at myself for hoping things would be different this time, even though I'd been sneaking around night after night.

My feet pounded on the pavement, and the sweat poured off me. I wasn't quite used to running in the Australian heat. I pulled my shirt over my head, tucking it into the waistband of my shorts without even slowing my pace.

As I ran, I pondered on whether I'd be able to stay and work with Matt in a completely platonic way. I decided I probably could if I kept it in the forefront of my mind about him never coming out.

My mind wandered to Samantha. Would she go with him on tour? Would I have to watch them both together every day? Could I even do that?

I took in my surroundings and realized I was back at the house. Unable to face going back inside right then, I paused on the driveway and did some stretches to let my overused muscles cool down.

"It's good to see you. Dom was worried you might be quitting on us already," Kat joked, totally unaware of how close to home that statement might be. She was coming from where the trash cans were kept, so I could only assume she'd been putting the trash out when she stumbled upon me in the driveway.

"No." The word left my mouth instantly, and I knew I wouldn't give this chance up willingly. If this last couple of weeks had shown me anything, it was that I was excited to get back into the music, and I wanted to see if I could enjoy it as much as Matt, Dom, and Kat seemed to. "I just needed to clear my head."

"Good, because we'd miss you." She stepped forward and opened her arms as if she were going to hug me but quickly stepped back, a grimace on her face. "I'm gonna go distract Dom while you go sneak into the shower because I am not sitting with you in that garage for the next god only knows how many hours while you stink like that."

I sniffed at myself and chuckled as I nodded in agreement. "Yeah, I guess I could use a shower."

"Could?" she stated, shaking her head in disbelief. "Right, give me two minutes to clear the way before you come in."

I mock saluted. "Yes, ma'am."

I'm not sure how Kat did it, but by the time I entered the house, it was free of everyone. After grabbing some clean clothes from the bedroom, I headed straight for the shower to freshen up.

CHAPTER THIRTY-SEVEN

SAM

AIMEE and I left the others—minus Will, who Kat insisted was in the shower—in the garage to do band stuff, and just like we did every day, we both made our way to the backyard to our little writing haven.

The house and garden were on a hill which meant from the lawn, there was a beautiful view of the mountains in the distance. We'd set up a couple of lounge chairs under the shade of one of those large umbrellas and got started with our morning routine. We'd put on some muse-inspiring tunes— usually of the country music variety—open up our documents and let our fingers tap away until they cramped up. Unless we were unlucky and hit a scene that brought us to a stop because we couldn't figure out how to get from point A to point B. The latter was usually my problem. Aimee was more than happy to jump from one scene to another, even if there were three scenes missing between them. I couldn't get my head around that, but it worked for her.

"Okay. Let's do this. And… *go!*" Aimee called out, starting our twenty-minute writing sprint. A lot of authors found sprints worked best for getting the words down. You gave yourself a timeframe and used it to focus solely on knocking the words out. No Facebook, no internet scrolling, just adding words to that blank page.

"Gone," I answered, and I stared at the cursor flashing on my screen.

I was supposed to be writing a sex scene between my two main characters, but all I could think about was Matt's reaction this morning when Dom knocked on the door. From the way he'd been every night the three of us had been fooling around and even the way he'd spoken about Will previously, I'd never have guessed he was that scared of Dom knowing about his sexuality. He clearly loved Will, so how could he not want to share that with the world? I just didn't understand his logic.

After Will had left, Matt was quick to excuse himself to the bathroom under the guise that he wanted a shower, but he'd not taken anything with him. When he returned without wet hair, I could only assume he'd just needed the time to himself.

When he came back, he didn't mention anything to do with Will. He just announced that Dom had called the band to the garage, which meant they'd be in there for at least the next few hours.

I was under no illusion, knew I'd fallen in love with Matt, but I was also attracted to Will and was on my way to falling for him too. After all the nights the three of us had shared, I'd thought we'd maybe be able to have something special between the three of us, long term. Unfortunately, after Matt's actions that morning, I couldn't see that happening now. Will had done the right thing walking away. He deserved to be shown off, not hidden away. It didn't mean I wasn't disappointed about him walking away, though. Part of me wished he'd stuck around and fought for himself and fought for what we'd had and could have. I wanted to stand up and fight for the three of us, but I had no right to do that. This was about them, and they had a history that only they could speak of.

"Why can't I hear your keyboard clicking?" Aimee asked, pulling me from my thoughts.

I huffed. "It sounds like you're doing enough clicking for the both of us."

Aimee gave me a pointed look. "It doesn't work like that, and you know it. What's up?"

I wanted to talk my problems through with her. She was my best friend, but these problems stemmed from Matt's issues, and they weren't mine to tell, especially when it was things he didn't want his best friend and her boyfriend to know. "It's not really my problem, and it's not my place to talk about it," I said with a shake of my head. The wounded look she gave me tugged at my heartstrings, but that didn't change anything. "I'm sorry. You know if it were something to do with me, you'd be the first person I'd talk it through with."

Aimee reached over the arms of the chairs and squeezed my forearm. "I know. I guess I'm feeling a little distanced from you since I came back. I know it's my own doing because I've been spending every second with Dom—"

"Hey, I'm just as bad with Matt, and Will, since they are thick as thieves," I interjected, not wanting her to blame herself for something we were both guilty of.

She gave me a weak smile. "I'm hoping these writing sessions will get us back to what we were before the accident."

I nodded. "In more ways than one." Neither of us had had a good writing session since then, and we both wanted to live off these businesses we were building. We couldn't get there without the words.

Aimee's phone started ringing, causing us both to jump. She swiped at the screen. "Ugh. Looks like time's up. Since neither of us has anything worth tallying up, let's start with a fresh sprint."

"Sounds good to me and my big fat zero," I said with a chuckle.

Aimee made a show of cracking her knuckles. "Okay… ready?" She lifted her eyes to mine.

I gave her a firm nod as I told myself I meant business. I needed to let my concerns about Matt and Will fall away for now so I could focus on the characters on my screen and their drama.

"*Go!*" Aimee called out.

I placed my fingers on the keyboard, and within seconds, I fell into a fiction world and someone else's story. It felt good. More than that, I was once again doing what I loved.

CHAPTER THIRTY-EIGHT

MATT

MY EYES KEPT STRAYING from the guitar in my hand and landing on Will and his long, slender fingers currently strumming the strings on his guitar—fingers that had been wrapped around my cock last night and plenty of others over places the last couple of weeks. At the time, I'd imagined the three of us going on like that forever, but now I knew that wouldn't be the case, and we'd probably never get a repeat of that again.

"*Matt!*" Dom commanded while clicking his fingers. I flicked my eyes to his, and the concern I could see in them told me he'd been trying to get through to me for some time.

I shook my head. "I'm sorry. What did you say?"

Dom placed his guitar in the stand beside the chair. "Let's take a break. It's almost lunchtime, anyway."

Kat jumped up excitedly. "Good idea. I'm starving."

"I'll make some sandwiches," Al stated as he followed Kat out the door leading into the house with Dom walking alongside him.

"I'm gonna check on the girls and see if they're ready for a break, too." Dom threw me a look over his shoulder. "Are you coming?"

"Matt, can I just have a quick word first?"

I frowned at Will's request and shrugged at Dom. "We'll catch up." I watched Dom leave and the door close behind him before turning to face Will. I hadn't spoken to him since he'd walked out earlier in the morning. As much as I wanted to explain myself at that time, I didn't think it would even make a difference to the situation now because he was right when he said my closet status would never change.

"Look, Matt, the three of us… it was a mistake." My heart fractured at his words, causing a lump to form in my throat. "We should never have jumped into that situation without discussing it in depth first. While I was on my run, I realized I want to make this band venture work. I don't want our mistakes and what happened this morning to make things awkward between us." He paused, and I looked at him blankly, unsure what he wanted from me or even if he wanted a response.

"You were here first, and obviously you'll stay no matter what, but I need to know now before I get my heart set on this. Will you be able to put what happened behind us and keep working with me in the band? Or should I leave now?"

The band had hit it big without him, but I knew with his and Al's return, it could be even bigger and better, and we'd been writing music that we wanted again. Music we loved. Fuck, there was nothing worse than producing and releasing sounds we hated.

I chased him away from this life once. I wouldn't do it again.

"No, we can work together and hopefully stay friends. I still want that. What's happened hasn't changed that."

Will searched my face with bright blue eyes for a long moment before nodding. "Okay," he stated as he walked past me and out the door.

We'd had the roller door up partway to let the air flow

through, so I pressed the button on the wall to close it before some passerby stumbled upon our unattended instruments while we ate. I didn't know how Gary had managed it, but shortly after the guys had gotten settled here in the Jonas's house, a big ass truck turned up with all our instruments from home. He'd obviously had them flown in on the same flight as the guys, I understood that much. I just wasn't sure how he got my instruments since, as far as I knew, they were locked in my mom's garage—which was turned into my music room years ago—after I'd organized for them to be moved there from the tour bus when I'd made arrangements to fly with Sam. And I was the only one with a key, since it was given back to me before I flew out. Gary promised me Mom's garage was safe and locked up tight. I didn't want to look too deeply into the situation, so I tried not to think about it.

I found everyone sitting around the dining table, Aimee and Sam's laptops closed and pushed into the center. That told me they'd moved back inside from where they'd started their writing session outside. The sun had probably gotten too much for them after the first hour. We didn't have air conditioning in the garage, but when we opened the roller door, a nice breeze blew right through to the door that led out to the yard.

Sam held an arm out to guide me to her as I approached the table, so I stopped to press a quick kiss to the top of her head before heading to the kitchen for food.

"The plate in the fridge is yours," Al called out as I reached for the refrigerator door.

"Thanks, Al." Al had become the self-appointed chef. He'd made most of us breakfast this morning and now sandwiches for lunch. It shouldn't surprise me since he was a great cook. You'd often find him helping his mom with the Sunday roast. And I knew he'd helped out a time or two in the cafe that Kat often worked at when we were home too.

Sam had saved an empty seat beside her, and I pressed my lips against hers as I slid in without much thought. It was only when I lifted my eyes to see Will watching us that my heart constricted in my chest. How the hell were we going to act like nothing had happened when every time I saw him, I thought about what we'd done together? I couldn't help wondering if I were naïve all along to think I could just fix our friendship and forget about what we once were to each other?

Sam squeezed my thigh, and I pulled my attention from Will to her. "Are you okay?"

"He's been distracted all morning. I was worried you two had had a lover's tiff or something," Dom announced, making me cringe at the thought of everyone noticing something had been up with me.

"You're such a drama queen. I'm just dwelling on the fact that what was meant to be a holiday has quickly turned into all work and no play," I offered, hoping that excuse was enough to get everyone off my back.

To be honest, it was partly true. I'd expected to have a few weeks here to spend time getting to know the beautiful girl beside me—the girl who I'd fallen in love with—and maybe seeing some of what Australia had to offer while I was here. I hadn't, for one second, expected to spend most of my days in a stuffy garage with four other people writing our next album. That was what our time had turned into. We did try to have a couple of days where we only had fun, but as we fell into our creative spaces, it was hard to give ourselves the time for fun.

CHAPTER THIRTY-NINE

SAM

MATT HAD SEEMED off all day long. We'd not gotten any time to ourselves to discuss what happened earlier in the morning, so I had no idea what he was thinking about it all or even where we stood now. I think everyone could tell something was wrong, but nobody knew what to ask.

Obviously, Dom being Matt's best friend, kept asking, "What the fuck is wrong with you?" But Matt just kept brushing it off with bullshit excuses that nobody seemed to fall for, but they didn't press him further.

I'd come to bed about an hour ago, expecting Matt to join me quickly since he hadn't been in a social mood today, but he seemed to be taking his damn sweet time. While I waited for him to join me in bed, I thought about what I would say to get to the bottom of things because I didn't want to go through another day like today—a day of not knowing what the hell was going on. The only thing I was certain of was the fact that Will probably wouldn't be sneaking in here with us again.

Finally, Matt slipped into the room on light feet, gently closing the door behind him with barely any noise, obviously expecting me to have already fallen asleep.

The idea pissed me off.

Was that why he'd taken so long to come to bed, to avoid even speaking to me?

The sound of clothing rustling told me he was stripping down to get in bed, so I laid still pretending to be asleep. The air hit my bare skin as the covers lifted, and the bed depressed as he settled next to me, leaving a gap, so he wasn't even touching me, which wasn't like him at all. Other nights, even when I'd gone to bed first, he'd always pulled me against his front and pressed a kiss to my cheek.

My stomach churned at the possible meaning behind his lack of actions. I couldn't lie still any longer, so I turned on him. "Are you going to explain what's going on, or do I need to jump to my conclusions, and let me tell you what you're giving me right now isn't giving me any nice ones," I said, faking a calm I didn't feel as tears welled in my eyes. I was more than grateful he couldn't see them in the darkness of the room. I didn't want him to be guilted into anything by my emotions.

Matt took in a deep breath, and I couldn't tell if it was to calm himself or simply to give himself an extra couple of seconds to think through what he was going to say. I focused on just listening to his words and his voice as he opened his mouth, knowing those were the only things I could go on in the dark. "Nothing is going on. Will and I spoke, and we agreed what happened between the three of us doesn't have to change anything."

My eyebrows hit my hairline. "What? You and Will chatted? I know you both have history, but since I was somewhat involved these last few weeks and thought if there were a future in that, I'd be part of it, and my opinion would at least matter for something." I'd been angry before, but now my blood was boiling. If my opinion was that unimportant to him, and Will for that matter, this conversation was over.

It was all over.

I wasn't going to spend another minute in bed with him.

I shoved at his chest and moved to turn back around, but his hands locked on my wrists, tugging my arms to pull me against him and trapping them between us.

"*Sammy!*" His voice was soft and gentle, but I wasn't going to be that weak and let the fight fall from me that quickly. I kept my body stiff against his as I ground my teeth together. "Of course, your opinion matters. It's just… Will was right this morning when he said I hadn't changed. I can't be with him without hiding who we are. I know that makes me a coward, but—" He growled in frustration as I felt his body shake, making me think he was shaking his head. "There's no 'but'. I *am* a coward. I'm sorry we didn't involve you in our conversation, but I love you, and nothing between the two of us has to change unless you can't bring yourself to love a coward like me."

My anger dissipated immediately, and I relaxed against him, pressing my forehead against his chest. I was disappointed and felt lost knowing we wouldn't have something with Will. I was falling for him, but that didn't mean anything had changed about my feelings toward Matt. "I love you, too, Matt. You being scared won't change that. Ever." I pressed a kiss to his chest, right over his heart.

We laid in silence as Matt's hand stroked up and down my spine causing goosebumps to break out on my body. As much as I loved him, I needed him to know that I was genuinely attracted to Will, and although they'd agreed just to forget and try for friends or bandmates, I might struggle to accept that at first.

"You and Will have had years to get used to not being together even though you both harbor feelings for each other. And I know I was only with you both for a few short weeks, but there was a connection between the three of us that I've never felt before. It might take me time to accept that it's just the two of us."

Matt's fingers brushed against my chin, tilting my head enough for him to press a kiss to my lips before pulling back just a fraction. "That's understandable. But we were working just fine before Will arrived, and I'm sure we can get back to that in time. I'll give you as much as you need." He pressed another kiss to my mouth, and after one swipe of his tongue against my seam, I went compliant beneath him. I wanted him.

Whether I wanted Will as well, it didn't matter. That was no longer a possibility. I wouldn't want to give up Matt for anything, and I proceeded to show him that in the best way I could.

CHAPTER FORTY

MATT

SAM DIDN'T TAKE LONG to drift off to sleep after we'd shown each other what our hearts felt. I loved the feel of her soft, relaxed body wrapped in my arms. Every night, the second I got into bed, I slid in behind her and ensured she was embraced in my arms. She never complained even when she'd been asleep. She'd simply press a kiss against the bicep across her chest and muttered a 'night.' Tonight we were in the same position, but my heart wasn't elated. It was breaking because I knew this was the last time I'd ever hold her like this.

I'd be leaving before sunrise, never to return.

I loved her with my whole being, and because of that, I had to let her go. She'd made it clear she had an attraction to Will, just like I did, and it was my fault she couldn't explore that. If we stayed together, she'd have to deal with that every single day. If she came to America with me and joined us on tour, he'd be right in front of her but totally unreachable. I couldn't make her live like that. At least if I left now, she'd get a clean break, and once she was over us she'd be able to find someone who could give her everything she wanted.

Everything she deserved.

I backed out of bed as gently as possible, only releasing my breath when I knew for sure I hadn't disturbed Sam's sleep. Glancing around the room, I was suddenly grateful that I'd been living out of my suitcase because that meant I didn't have to dig around in closets for my clothes. Zipping my case closed every morning was also a blessing because I was fairly sure that noise would wake up Sam for sure.

I felt sick with guilt as I walked through the silent house. I shouldn't be scuttling away in the middle of the night. I should be thanking the Jonas's for allowing me to stay and giving them all hugs goodbye. Hell, Sam deserved an explanation, but this way, she'd at least hate me and therefore get over this so much quicker than the pain it would cause if I stayed to explain myself. Nothing would change, and I'd still be leaving because, at the end of the day, I couldn't make Sam live through the pain I'd been living for years all because I'm a coward.

No. This is for the best for everyone.

———

When I landed in New York, I turned my phone on, and within seconds, it was blowing up with notifications. Most of them from Dom and a couple from the other guys. Knowing I had to face the music sooner or later and feeling safe enough with all the miles between us, I pulled his contact up and pressed call.

"Matt. What the fuck?" Dom's voice was full of disbelief.

"Sorry. I had to leave. I—"

"Hang on, buddy." His voice went muffled, and I could just hear him excuse himself to somebody in the background. A second or two passed, and he was back, his voice as clear as ever. "Right, I'm on my own now. What's going on?"

I told him the only thing I thought he wouldn't delve too

far into. "Sam and I would never work long term. Neither of us could handle the distance. So I needed to leave before either of us fell too hard and couldn't survive the end." I swallowed past the lump in my throat. At that moment, I knew it was too late. I'd already fallen, and there was no surviving losing Sam.

It was something that would haunt me forever.

It was like I was repeating my own mistakes.

Only this time, I was letting the two loves of my life go.

CHAPTER FORTY-ONE

WILL

I RAN a hand over my face as I stepped out of the bedroom, hoping to make sense of what I thought I could see so early in the morning. Dom was pacing the dining room as Aimee held Sam in a comforting hug.

"Dom will get to the bottom of it." I heard her promise as she watched Dom with a worried gaze. It almost seemed as if she didn't believe her own words.

"What's going on?" I asked.

Dom pulled the phone from his ear and stabbed at the screen with his finger before putting it back to his ear. "Isn't that the million-dollar question?" he said with a humorless laugh.

I gave him a blank look, waiting for him to fill in the blanks, but he just kept up with the same jabbing at his phone and then putting it back to his ear.

"Matt's left. Gone back to New York, I assume." Sam's voice was small, and I hated hearing it like that. She hadn't seemed weak for even one second since I met her, but now being held by her best friend, I just wanted to wrap her in my arms.

"Fuck!" Dom slammed his phone on the table, and I cringed at the high probability of it being broken. Although Dom no doubt had the money to replace a broken phone, being a rockstar and all.

Sam stepped back out of Aimee's hold. "He slipped out during the night. He's probably in the air. I'm sure when he sees all your missed calls, he'll return them." She brushed past me and reached for her bedroom door. "I'm gonna—" she stopped mid-sentence.

I placed my hand on her shoulder and gave it a firm squeeze. "Take five minutes for yourself to think. That's what you're going to do while I make you a coffee."

Sam stepped out from under my hand and disappeared into her room. As I headed for the coffee machine, I noticed Aimee watching Sam's closed door, her brow furrowed with worry. I hadn't known Sam half as long as Aimee had, and I was concerned too.

What the hell was Matt thinking?

———

"Come in," Sam called after I knocked on the bedroom door.

I had a muffin on a plate in one hand and a coffee in the other. I glanced around and caught Aimee's eyes. "Could you…" I nodded to the door.

She smiled. "Sure." Reaching around me, she opened the door and nudged me in. I expected her to take a moment to check on Sam, but once I was in, I heard the door close behind me with a click. I was very aware it was just Sam and me in the room.

Sam was sitting on the bed, her back against the headboard, her messy bun pressed against the wall, and her eyes closed. I stopped beside her, unsure of whether to disturb her or not. I wouldn't say she looked at peace, not with the slight furrow in her forehead and her lips tightly pressed together, but she definitely looked like she was deep in thought.

She cracked open an eye and took in the plate. "I appreciate the trouble you went to, but I don't think I can stomach anything right now."

"That's okay. I'll leave the muffin here, and if you get hungry later, it's right there waiting for you," I suggested, placing the plate on the bedside table.

I walked around the bed and mirrored her position against the headboard. I kept quiet, knowing if I were in her place, I'd be grateful for the company but wouldn't want someone to start telling me what they thought without actually asking them about it.

"I can't believe he ran out in the middle of the night," she uttered in the quiet room. "I thought we had something special."

I placed my hand on her knee to comfort her. "I know I've not seen you guys together long, but from what I have seen over the last couple of weeks, you do have something special. Don't ever doubt that."

She nodded in acknowledgment, and I watched as a tear trailed down her cheek. "I just wish I knew why. If he didn't think he could tell me to my face, surely, he could've left me a note. It's the least I deserve."

I couldn't help but feel like I was the catalyst in all this. If I'd never stepped foot on Australian soil, Matt wouldn't have left as he did. I wanted to fix this for Samantha. Hell, for them both, but I wasn't sure I could. I knew for certain that I couldn't even try while I was still here. I needed to go home and speak to Matt face to face to get to the bottom of things. I'd thought we'd sorted it all out when we spoke in the garage, but clearly, I read that situation wrong. I'd been doing a lot of that lately.

"I'm going to change my flight and go speak with Matt," I told her, having come to the only conclusion I could live with.

She turned to look at me, her brows drawn in a frown. "You can't do that. You're here to bond with the band and write your album. You still have a week left."

I shrugged. "A fifth of the band is missing, and that fifth is half the writing team. So, the album isn't going to be written here anymore."

"Huh… I guess that makes sense." She sighed and flicked her gaze away from mine. "He still loves you, you know?"

I didn't want to admit it out loud because acknowledging that broke my heart a little more, but it was obviously true after how he'd reacted while the three of us were intimate these last weeks. But like Sam said, she deserved the truth, even about this. "He does, but not enough. Asking him to come out to the world, although it is a *huge* thing, I don't think it's asking too much in the grand scheme of things."

Sam placed her hand on top of mine, and I twisted my hand beneath hers, curling my fingers so we were holding hands. "It isn't. Not at all. A love like what you two have for each other shouldn't be hidden away from the world."

Her words warmed my heart, and I offered her a grateful smile.

"Promise me you'll do whatever it takes to get the happiness you both deserve?"

"I will," I promised, knowing that the only way to get that would be to have Sam in both our lives. We'd never work as a couple, not after the three of us. Sam was just as much our soul mate as we were to each other. We were a destined 'throuple' if that was even a word.

CHAPTER FORTY-TWO

MATT

I STARED at the four walls of what was once my childhood bedroom but now a generic guest bedroom. I didn't blame my mom for redecorating at all—the plan had been that after our tour, I was going to buy my own place. It was just that Australia happened, and my search got a little delayed. I'd honestly not even thought about it once while I was away. Now, though, I decided it was most definitely my top priority.

There was a light tapping on the door. "Matt, are you awake? Someone is here asking to see you."

My heart thumped in my chest.

Could it be Sam?

Could she have followed me back?

"He doesn't look anything like the person he says he is, so I shut the door in his face. But he hasn't left yet, so maybe he isn't lying about his identity."

I shook my head at my stupid thoughts jumping straight to Sam. She didn't even know my parents' address, so she'd be the last person to turn up here. She probably hated me for leaving as I did, which was exactly what I'd been aiming for when I left, so I shouldn't be pining over her right now. "I'm coming."

Mom still stood outside my bedroom door when I opened it. She offered me a shrug as she led the way to the front door.

"Who did he say he was?"

"Will Sibree. But this guy is broad and tattooed. He doesn't even resemble the sweet kid Will was."

I laughed. "Mom, people do grow up, you know." My brow furrowed as I wondered if it really was Will. His flight wasn't due back for another couple of days. Gary had booked Will, Kat, and Al's flights to return a few days earlier than Dom's and mine, since he had no idea what our itineraries were, and no matter how much he asked us about them, we were not letting it slip.

I pulled the front door open ready to blast whoever it was, but as soon as I laid eyes on Will, I closed my mouth without uttering a word.

"Hey," he offered. He seemed unsure, no doubt wondering if he was doing the right thing by being here. My eyes roamed down his body on their own accord. He was casually dressed in sweats and a t-shirt, and then my gaze drifted to the suitcase at his feet.

"You came straight from the airport?" I asked him with a wide-eyed stare.

Will nodded, causing the longer parts of his blond hair to bounce on top of his head. "I had to. What was going on in your head? Why did you leave?"

I glanced behind me to make sure Mom wasn't eavesdropping and then quickly pulled the door closed. I didn't need her to get on my back about settling down with a girl, not now that I knew it wouldn't be happening. Ever. Nobody would fill the Sam-sized hole in my heart.

"I did what was best for everyone."

"How the hell do you figure that? You left Sam without a

word of explanation. She's destroying herself trying to work out where you guys went wrong." Will sighed like he was disappointed. "She thinks she must have been the only one to feel like what you had was special."

Just the idea that she was thinking made my heart hurt. I swallowed past the lump in my throat. "She wasn't, but if she thinks that, she'll maybe move on quicker."

"I don't understand. What I saw of you two, you were a great couple meant for each other." There was a longing tone behind his words, and I couldn't help but feel that same longing too. The three of us were meant for each other.

I didn't have Sammy in my life for long, but I now knew those days would be the happiest of my life.

Will ran a hand through his blond locks, and mine itched to follow. "I can see you've made up your mind, even if I do think it's the wrong decision and you're going to live to regret it." He bent and grabbed his suitcase and left me to chew on those ominous words.

———

I HAD a peaceful couple of days after Will left. Dom had seemingly given up on calling or messaging me, and I only received two calls from Kat—one to tell me she and Al had both returned home, and if I wanted to hang out, I'd be more than welcome to visit them, and then a second a couple of days later telling me Dom had come home early. He'd apparently gone straight to his room and not made another appearance. According to Kat, their mom, Rosa, was acting strange as though she knew what was happening but wouldn't talk about it.

What a bunch of silent brooders we all seem to be. As much as I was gutted things hadn't worked out between Dom and Aimee like we'd all thought they would, I was a little happy he'd be distracted enough not to be on my back about up and leaving Australia like I did. I knew I should touch base and offer him my condolences, but I was also well aware of what it was like to want to be alone and deal with shit by yourself and in your own way.

Since I'd been back home, my parents and I had been binge-watching the television show *Vikings* in the evening, and by day, Mom and I were working our way through all the rom-coms Netflix had to offer while my dad went to work. It was such a nice change to chill with my parents, even if we'd never been as loving as the Saxtons.

When the band got signed, we were rushed away to record an album, and then we had to promote the album, which turned into a long-ass tour. It was all such a manic change in my early adult life, and at the time, I hadn't realized how much I'd missed my mom and dad. We hadn't been very close-knit before I left, but now that I was home, it was hitting me how much I had missed them. I was most definitely going to make the most of my time with them before the chaos of the band started all over again with the next album. It was only going to be a matter of time now all of us were back on American soil.

Thoughts of Sam were constantly there in the back of my mind, but I pushed them away until they were like a whisper in the breeze.

CHAPTER FORTY-THREE

WILL - ONE MONTH LATER

I WAS JUST FINISHING up a tattoo on David, one of my regular clients, when the shop's phone rang. I didn't stop my work to answer the line, knowing with multiple handsets in the shop, someone else would pick up. It would most likely be Kelsey, who worked our front desk.

I wiped at the dragon on the man's arm and sat back taking in my work. I swelled with pride. The joy I got from bringing people's tattoo ideas to life by inking them on their skin as a permanent marking was something I didn't think I could replicate doing with anything else. The amazement on their faces when they saw it was always the icing on the cake, so I watched him closely as I told him it was done.

He flicked his eyes down to look at his upper arm, but because the dragon wrapped around it, I knew he wouldn't get the whole picture without a mirror.

"Go check it out in the mirror while I get the wrappings together." I pointed to the mirror on the back of the door and watched him out the side of my eye as I went about what I was doing.

"Oh my god. It's fantastic." He stepped so close to the

mirror that he was almost touching it. "The colors. The detail. Those scales are…" He turned his head in a sharp motion to face me. "Man, you're amazing."

A grin spread across my face as that pride I'd felt earlier doubled. "I'm glad you're happy with it."

"Happy? I'm ecstatic, man! I'll be sending all my friends your way." He'd turned back to the mirror, and his eyes trailed over the reflection of the dragon.

I cleared my throat. "Yeah, about that. I love recommendations, but I'm going to be out of action for a while because…" I hated telling people about Running Hearts. It felt weird to think I was a member of a huge band. "Well, I'm going away to record an album and going on tour with a band for a while."

"Awesome. What band? Maybe I've heard of you guys." He headed back to the seat he'd been in for the last three hours and sat back down.

I poured some solution on a tissue and wiped it over his arm again. "The band's already been around, I'm just joining them. Again." He frowned, and I went on as I gently rubbed some cream over his new ink. "I was an original member of the band, Running Hearts, but when they hit it big, I wasn't ready for that kind of life." His eyes widened as he recognized the name, and I shrugged. "I simply wanted to open my shop and leave my mark on people in a different way."

We both laughed at that as I wrapped some clear wrap around his arm. Once I was done, I stood and directed him to the door. "Keep it clean. Don't get it too wet. Put cream on it a couple of times a day. And you shouldn't have any problems."

We walked out of my room and headed through to the front of the shop. I grabbed a card as we passed the front desk and handed it to him. "Any problems or questions don't hesitate to call. If I'm not here, the other guys are all super talented artists who would be more than happy to help you out."

David shoved the card in his jeans back pocket and took my hand in his, giving it a grateful shake. "Thanks. I'll definitely be back for more in the future, and your break will give me time to save for it. Good luck with everything."

"Thanks." I watched him leave. When the door closed behind him, I turned to Kelsey who was talking into the phone, her lips turned up in a happy smile.

"Okay. I'll let him know." Her smile spread to her eyes as she listened to the other person reply. "Yeah. You, too." She hung up and glanced at me, seeming a little shocked to see me there.

"What? You were so engrossed in your call you didn't even notice me come out with a client and say goodbye?" Her face flushed, and I knew I'd hit the nail on the head. "Jesus, Kels. Who's the lucky fella?"

"Shut up!" she said, turning away and placing the phone back in its charging dock. "It was Kat. She told me to tell you Gary is sending a car to her place to pick you all up on Monday to take you to the airport."

"The airport?" Could we be going back to Australia? My stomach somersaulted in excitement at the thought of seeing Sam again.

Kelsey glanced down at the book on the desk. "Yeah, he's flying you all out to LA to start recording. Apparently, Dom has some more songs already written, and Matt's been working on the melody."

"Shit. It's Saturday. I thought I'd at least have a week's notice before things kicked off." I could've punched myself for not keeping in touch with the guys more while being back the last couple of weeks. I'd dropped back into my normal life and simply assumed I'd have time before we all got back together to write. I didn't realize Dom and Matt would go it alone. In a way, that frustrated me because they wanted me as part of the band, but they weren't really treating me as such if they were too busy writing without me.

"Luckily, that was your last booking. I've been pushing new clients toward the other guys like you'd suggested when you first came back from Australia," she said, unaware of my thoughts.

I sighed. "Yeah, luckily." Part of me wished I was booked up for months, so I'd have an excuse to walk away from the band. Who was I kidding? Deep down, I wanted to be part of the band more than anything, and that was why I was so pissed about them writing without me.

Knowing I needed to talk to them in person, I went back to my room and made quick work of cleaning up. Once that was done, I grabbed my phone and called Al, hoping he'd be able to tell me where the rest of the guys were.

———

I PULLED off my helmet and hung it over the handlebars as I swung my leg over the tank of my bike. The door clattered, and light footsteps came down the driveway.

"Will." I caught Kat as she threw her arms around my neck. "I thought you'd backed out on us."

I laughed. "Nah, I don't think Gary would let that happen, not after I signed all those papers for him. He's probably got me locked into this for life." I placed her down and made a show of thinking, running a hand over my chin. "I probably should've gotten a lawyer to read over that first."

She slapped at my chest playfully. "You're an idiot."

"I would be if I signed over my firstborn."

She shook her head and grabbed my hand, pulling me toward the house. "Are the rest of the guys going to be as happy to see me?"

"Pfft. Happy? I don't think Matt or Dom know what that word even means anymore. Since coming back from Australia, they've been the most miserable I've seen them." She weighed me up for a second. "Wait, did Al tell you what happened between Dom and Aimee?"

I shook my head. All he'd told me was that they were miserable fuckers who had thrown themselves into making music. Angsty music about heartbreak at that. It wasn't like that was a problem since that shit sold well.

She passed with her hand on the front door and leaned toward me, lowering her voice. "Aimee had an abortion, and Dom's broken. We're all hoping he'll figure out a way to get past the grief because he's going to burn himself out if he keeps creating like he has been."

I didn't know Aimee well, but she loved Dom, and anyone could see it. It was so clear in the way she looked at him, even when she thought nobody was watching. I couldn't see her aborting his child. It seemed more like she'd treasure a child that was a part of him, especially after I'd seen how maternal she was with her own kids.

CHAPTER FORTY-FOUR

MATT - SIX MONTHS LATER

"THAT'S it for us tonight, folks. Big D, the main man you've been waiting for, will be rapping his heart out for you very soon. Thank you, and good night!" Dom called out into the microphone as I strummed the last few cords on my guitar.

The lights cut out, and we made our way offstage. One of the crew members unhooked me from all the wires and took away the guitar.

"Hey, Matty," Big D said as he came into view from wherever he'd been hiding during our show. "That was an awesome performance tonight. Let's hope I can give them just as good of one."

"I'm sure you will," I offered, knowing the audience would eat up everything he gave them. They were, after all, mainly his fans.

A couple of weeks ago, we'd been asked to help him out by stepping in to be his support act on his tour after the original band booked in had been let go due to a sexual assault case. It was initially meant to be for a couple of nights, but when his fans responded well to us, our manager decided it would be a good way to promote the new album and our upcoming tour.

"Darius, why are you not getting into position?" Sadie, Big D's personal representative, questioned, hands on her hips and giving him a look that told everyone no matter what his answer was, she wouldn't like it. Darius was an easy-going guy, so his pocket rocket of a PR was really good for keeping him on track.

D rolled his eyes and looked to his drummer dressed in a tank top, raggedy worn denim shorts, and a backward facing 'I love NYC' cap to keep his long spiky blond hair out of his face while he performed. "I guess Sadie isn't interested in keeping our support act happy, Kamil."

"No, they did their job, and Sadie would like you to do yours," Sadie offered. The fact that she was talking about herself in third person made me smile. Although she was always cracking the whip, she was amazing at her job, and I secretly wished we'd get someone equally as good when we started our tour in another month.

Darius turned his body into Kamil's and leaned in real close. "Kiss me quickly before she drags me away."

Kamil laughed and closed the distance between them, sliding his hands over Darius's butt and pulling their groins together as their mouths connected. The love they had was so obvious.

Jealousy flared within me as I tore my eyes away from the happy couple and looked everywhere but at them. *How could they be so open and honest with all those people around them? Watching them?* At times like that, I'm reminded of what I could have had if only I weren't so scared of what other people thought of me. I focused on the crew milling around, and although most of them were paying more attention to the jobs they were doing over the two men kissing, the little smiles they sent the couple's way weren't missed.

I wanted that so badly. I wanted to have someone waiting at the side of the stage after a gig. My mind went to a beautiful brunette who had once sat on a stool just like the one Sadie was currently perched on, offering me gentle touches and excited smiles every time I passed to get changed or swap out a guitar.

Sammy.

My mind always went to her, and even though it still made me sad because it was all my own fault, I threw away what we had, I could still think of her and enjoy the memories now, seven or eight months after I'd last seen her.

Dom was taking his last breakup a lot worse than me, even though it happened around the same time, but he lost a child in that breakup too, so I guessed it wasn't surprising, after all.

Will appeared at my side, and as Kamil and Darius gave us both a goodbye wave before running to get in position, I found myself wondering why I'd made our lives so miserable and lonely. Even though to the outside world, Will and I were as close as we used to be when we were best friends all those years ago, only we knew it was a front. We'd never get back to what we once were because I kept him at arm's length, too afraid to allow myself to enjoy his company in the ways we both wanted. Yeah, we both missed the person who brought us back together, and nothing would change that, but we missed each other too.

At that moment, I had an epiphany.

We couldn't go on like this, pretending to live a happy life when we were doing nothing of the sort.

I wanted what Darius and Kamil had.

I wanted to throw my arms around Will's neck as I came off stage and press my lips to his. Why the fuck should it matter who was watching or what they were thinking? As long as we were happy, everyone else could get fucked. It wasn't like the world was going to end because two guys showed who they were and loved. Darius and Kamil just proved that.

I let my fingers brush Will's and smirked as his eyes widened in surprise at my willing touch. "We need to talk, but I have to do something first. Wait for me here?" He nodded, and with a quick "I'll be back," I ran off to find the other person who meant the world to me but in a purely platonic way.

Dom was in the green room like I'd expected, lounging on a chair with a beer bottle in his hand. He hadn't drunk any. Like always, he just nursed it, which seemed like a complete waste to me. He cracked an eye open as he heard me enter, but after seeing it was me, he once again relaxed. With neither of us being in happy places lately, we'd fallen into a pattern of just chilling together in a silent cloud of misery. Not tonight, though. I needed to tell him who I really was. Because if I couldn't be honest with my best friend, how could I even think of being honest with the rest of the world?

"Dom, we need to talk."

Dom sighed. "If this is the start of that intervention Kat has been threatening me with, I'm walking and never coming back."

Shit! I didn't realize things had gotten so bad that neither of them was willing to go to such lengths to move forward. Dom's words cemented the idea that this was the right step to making things better, especially if the band had been in such a vulnerable state, and I had been too blind in my own misery to see it.

"It's not about you even though whatever Kat has been saying is probably right. This is about me." I wrung my hands together as my stomach churned.

"Go on, then, I'm listening," he offered as he straightened in his seat.

"Fuck, I don't know where to start."

Dom frowned as he looked at me, closer than he'd looked at me in a long time, his frown deepening the longer he looked and the more he saw. We'd both been living with blinkers on for the last eight months, and it clearly wasn't healthy for anyone.

I took a deep breath and rushed the words out quickly before I could chicken out, "I'm bisexual. I've been in love with Will since we were teenagers."

A small smile played over his lips. "It's about damn time."

I struggled to swallow around my dry throat. "What do you mean?"

"I've been waiting for the day when you'd finally come out and admit who you are."

I stared at him in stunned disbelief.

He'd known all this time?

He laughed, no doubt at whatever he could see on my face and stood before walking over to me. "Close your mouth. You look like a damn fish." He patted me on the arm and pulled me into a manly hug. "Did you really think I didn't know? You're like a brother to me, and I can read you damn well." He pulled back and offered me a loving smile. "I knew you were hooking up with Will back in the day… Your secret looks at each other and then both disappearing together at parties. I was so jealous at first. I felt left out until it clicked, and I realized what was going on. I might love you both, but yeah, not like that."

We both chuckled before he quickly sobered again. "Sam? Did she find out about your past and not like it? I guess it could've been hard knowing an ex was still in your life and only going to become more active in it."

I shook my head. "God, no. Sam was amazing. I told her about my past with Will even before there was talk of him doing the band again. She got it. She got me." The usual pang in my chest hit me as I thought about what I'd lost walking away from her.

"Then what happened between you two?"

I blew a breath out of my mouth while I thought about how to explain my cowardice without him thinking less of me. "I fucked up," I told him. I could see that now. No matter how much I thought walking away was the best thing for everyone at the time, I now knew it wasn't.

Dom stared at me while I worked through my thoughts, and I finally told him everything. From the three of us getting closer and spending night after night together to the freak-out I had the day he knocked on the door.

"So, you left Sam because you didn't want her to come back with you and see Will every day, and then be left wanting more with the three of you." I nodded. "You thought she'd leave you eventually, so you walked first."

When I heard him say the words and the disbelief behind them, I felt stupid because as much as he was right, in my thoughts, Sam would never have left me because of that.

"Like I said, I fucked up, and there's no way of fixing it. I have no way of contacting her. I don't even know the street address to go old-school and write a letter."

"What about social media? She's an author, so she's got to have it all. Surely, you could hit her up in a DM."

"And risk the exposure of that to the press from one lucky hack. No way." I grimaced at the thought.

Dom shrugged. "Gary would love a scandal getting out and having Running Hearts trending on all the socials."

I shook my head reverently. "And Gary can fuck off. I'm ready to come out to you and the guys. I'm not exactly ready to deal with the world's reaction just yet. Gary isn't milking a scandal from my life."

I'd probably never be able to fix things with Sam, but Will

was another story. Even if he'd never forgive me for what I did to Sam and didn't want to try things with just the two of us, we both deserved the truth, and I needed my truth out there.

CHAPTER FORTY-FIVE

WILL

I WAITED by the stage like a freaking idiot for god knows how long. The only saving grace was that at least I had a front-row seat to an amazing show by Darius. I could see why Big D had gotten such a big following. He was fucking brilliant. His lyrics were so relatable, even to me. And I'd never been a fan of rap music. I was more of a country guy. Hence, why when we originally got the band together, that was the lane we were heading in. Thankfully, that was also the way the band had gone since I joined up again. As much as I didn't mind their previous sound, what we sang now had so much more heart, even if most of it was currently about heartbreak and pain.

A hand fell on my shoulder, making me jump, and I turned to find Matt, his eyes sparkling with determination. He stepped close to me, so close I felt the need to move backward, but I fought the urge. The look on his face had me intrigued. Although we'd gotten our friendship back on track over the last few months, there was a huge wall between us, but this felt so different, I wanted to know what he was thinking.

"I had an epiphany earlier," he started. I nodded in

acknowledgment, not wanting to ruin his train of thought. "I've been an idiot. Because I love you. "

My heart leaped in my chest as he carried on speaking. I'd never thought I'd hear those three words from him.

"I've loved you since we were kids fooling around. I just wasn't brave enough to prove it."

His last sentence made me quirk a brow. "And you're brave enough now?"

His eyes dropped to my lips, and that's all the warning I got before he crushed his mouth against mine in a kiss full of passion and love. I heard the whispers around us backstage, and I broke the kiss in a panic. "Matt, people are watching."

"I don't care. Let them," he said before once again taking my lips with his. I gasped in shock, and he took advantage by pushing his tongue inside my mouth. I groaned as it stroked mine and grasped his hips with my hands, pulling his groin against mine. I felt his cock harden against mine and ground against him.

A throat cleared behind us.

Matt didn't jump back as I'd expected, so I pulled back, breaking the kiss and weighed him up.

"What?" he asked, a smile playing on his lips.

"Have you two finished sucking face yet? Because I'm pretty sure the band is long overdue a celebration," Dom stated from behind Matt.

Matt laughed and slapped me on the chest as he stepped back. "Stop looking so worried. I told you I was brave enough to prove I love you."

Dom nodded. "Come on, love birds, let's go find Kat and Al. Kat's gonna love this," he offered, pointing between the two of us.

Us. It had been months since I thought we had a chance at being a thing, and now here we were, Matt being open and out with me. Just like I'd dreamed. The thought of Sam flitted through my mind, but when Matt pressed a quick peck against my lips before tugging me, his hand wrapped in mine to follow Dom.

I'd been lost for years, just floating along with the wind, but now that Matt was holding my hand and kissing me in public, I was finally tethered.

CHAPTER FORTY-SIX

SAM

As I sat on the plane and watched Aimee try to settle Thea as the flight took off and her little ears popped, I wondered if we were doing the right thing. Dom deserved to know he had a daughter, and Aimee had searched for so long to find a way to contact him that giving this a go was the best and only way.

Once Aimee found out she was pregnant and realized how she'd only be repeating history having a child with a guy who would have no choice but to be a distant father, she felt her only option was an abortion. When Dom came to the conclusion that Aimee wasn't going to change her mind, he left the clinic, unable to watch the life being erased.

Aimee couldn't go through with it, though. And by the time she left the clinic, Dom was long gone.

She'd tried everything to get in touch with him but having been in each other's company twenty-four-seven since the accident, they hadn't exchanged numbers, just as I hadn't with Matt or Will. Even calling their manager, Gary, was of no use. All he wanted was for Aimee to disappear with a nice chunk of money he offered because Dom was writing the best songs of his life—full of pain and angst.

Obviously, Aimee didn't take the money, but it left her with no way to find Dom, so she settled down until she could figure something out.

When we got tickets for the red carpet event at the music awards show we were now heading to, she hoped it would be a way to talk to Dom.

I just prayed they'd hang around long enough for Aimee to catch Dom's attention, or else we'd be going back to the drawing board.

I knew deep down we were doing the right thing, but Aimee connecting with Dom meant I'd be seeing Matt and Will again.

Having followed them over the months via the media and whatever interviews I could find, I knew the tension between them had never gone. The fact that Matt had never tried to contact me again after walking out in the middle of the night, not even to give me an explanation as to why, had me harboring some anger toward him. I wasn't certain that I'd be able to spend two minutes in the same room as him without snapping. You never know, maybe he'd still want to avoid me and stay well away.

I couldn't decide if that was an option I preferred or not.

The guy beside me huffed. "I hope we won't have to put up with this for the whole flight," he grumbled to his wife beside him, not bothering to lower his voice as he glared past me toward Aimee and Thea.

We were in a four-seat row since it was a long flight, and Aimee needed a bassinet for Thea. Aimee bristled beside me, but she didn't stop murmuring soothingly to the upset baby in her arms to acknowledge the rude guy next to me.

My anger boiled, and I turned on him. "Look, she's doing all she can. Are your ears popping?"

He frowned. "Yeah?"

"Well, imagine you're a little baby who doesn't understand

what it is or why, just that it's uncomfortable and maybe even hurting." His face fell a little, and I hoped that meant he realized what a douche he was being. "Yeah, give them a goddamn break."

I shifted in my seat so my back was to the douchebag and offered Aimee a wicked grin when she met my eyes.

"Thank you," she mouthed while keeping up the gentle, rhythmic patting on Thea's bottom. Thea's cries had changed from ear-piercing whaling to an intermittent whine. Whether it was the comfort Aimee was offering or just that Thea was tiring herself out, I didn't know, but it didn't really matter. If it wouldn't stress both Aimee and Thea out, I'd like the crying to go on longer just to piss off the douchebag next to me.

An hour into the flight, Thea was well and truly out for the count, and Aimee was able to lay her in the bassinet that the flight attendant had set up once the seat belt sign went out.

We both took in turns to use the bathroom, and when I came back, the guy from the seat beside me was nowhere to be seen, and his wife was in his seat.

She gave me a small smile as I sat down. "I'm sorry about earlier." Her eyes flicked from mine to Aimee's over my shoulder, making it clear she was addressing us both.

I shook my head, but it was Aimee who spoke. "I don't need an apology from you, you did nothing wrong. It's your husband who should be apologizing."

She glanced nervously over the back of the chairs toward the bathrooms. "I know, but you deserve an apology, and I know my husband well enough to be aware that he won't give you one."

"That's on him, not you." The husband came back before anyone could say more. I was quite sure Aimee was done with the conversation, anyway, since she was already tucking her neck pillow into place and settling back in her seat to sleep.

My mind wasn't quite ready to shut off yet, so I slipped on the headphones and skimmed through the movies trying to find something that would entertain me for a while. Nothing jumped out at me, so accepting defeat, I turned off the screen and slid the headphones into the pocket on the wall in front of me.

"Is your mind running wild, too?" Aimee's voice made me jump. I'd thought she'd fallen asleep already.

"Shit." I placed a hand over my rapidly beating heart as I tried to calm my breaths down. "Yeah. My mind is more than a little busy. I'm guessing yours is probably worse, though. How are you feeling?"

Aimee shook her head as she stared at her daughter's sleeping form in the bassinet. "Nervous. Terrified. I know it's the right thing for Thea. Even if he doesn't want anything to do with me, he has the right to be in his daughter's life."

Typical Aims, always thinking of everyone else and what was good for them. She never put herself first. That was why I was here. I wanted to make sure she got what she needed. Even if she didn't get what she wanted, she'd get the support she'd need, no matter what.

Matt could ignore me. He could parade a squadron of girls in front of me, and I'd still stick around to support my best friend. That was one of the reasons I never told her about what happened between Matt, Will, and me, even though she had no idea Will was ever involved. She was going through so much with Dom and the pregnancy, I wasn't giving her more to worry about. By the time Thea arrived, it felt like so much time had passed that I didn't have a right to be bothered by it anymore. I should've moved on, 'should' being the operative word. I'd concluded that was something I'd never get over or even come to terms with. But it wasn't worth worrying my best friend over. If she ever found out, she'd feel betrayed I'd kept so much from her. To be honest, I was worried about how things would go down once we all ended up in the same room.

Would I be able to keep a lid on everything, or would it be a fruitless battle? I didn't know, but I was willing to risk it all to be there for my friend when she needed me most.

Even if it meant I'd be all alone when I needed someone to be there for me.

CHAPTER FORTY-SEVEN

MATT

DOM PACED the front room of his parents' house as we waited for Aimee and baby Thea to arrive. It was such a shock hearing she'd turned up at the awards night with a baby in tow, making it more than obvious she hadn't gone through with the abortion.

Just the thought of all that wasted time made me feel nauseous. I couldn't imagine what Dom was going through, thinking of all the things he'd missed throughout Aimee's pregnancy. Not that it was any fault of Aimee's, she'd apparently tried everything to get in touch with Dom. She'd even called Gary, who had offered to pay her off to stop trying to contact Dom. Obviously, she didn't take the money, but at that point, she knew she had no chance of getting to Dom via Gary.

"For fuck's sake, Dom, stop pacing. You're making me dizzy," Kat complained as she tugged on his arm and pulled him down to sit beside her on the sofa.

Dom ran a hand through his hair and tugged on the ends. "It's been a couple of days since I saw her. What if she changed her mind and went back to Australia?"

"Son, you said she spent the whole of her pregnancy trying to get in touch with you, so she isn't going to walk away now that she has found you," Rosa said as she took a seat on his other side and wrapped an arm around his shoulders.

There was a gentle knock on the door, and Dom jumped up from the chair and all but ran out the room in a rush to open the front door. Laughter filled the room, and Will squeezed my hand in his.

Ever since we'd kissed at Big D's concert a few weeks ago, we'd been openly dating. I hated myself for treating him like I did over the years, but it seemed like Will had forgiven me. He reminded me almost daily to look forward and remember past mistakes are in the past for a reason—learn and do better.

We'd spoken in length about Sam and tried to contact her via her social media pages speaking in code just in case someone else found them, but she never replied, so we assumed they'd gotten lost in her message request folder since they were never accepted or shown as read.

Now that Dom and Aimee were back in touch, I hoped we'd be able to contact Sam in other ways, but as much as I wanted to march up to her and demand Sam's cell number from her now, I'd promised Will I would at least give Dom and Aimee today before I did that.

"One more day, babe," Will reminded me, clearly knowing me well enough to know where my mind was. He pressed a chaste kiss to my mouth and pulled back as the sound of a baby's cry came closer.

Dom was our best friend and brother in every way but blood, and we were more than a little excited to meet our niece. Aimee had barely made it into the room when everyone surrounded her to get a look at the dark-haired bundle in her arms.

Dom turned on us all, blocking our access. "Guys… give them some space. You'll all get a cuddle."

"You can have one of Thea, too," Aimee joked, setting off a round of laughter that seemed to break the little tension that could be felt.

Aimee handed the crying bundle over to Dom, who was staring down at the baby with a mixed look of amazement and terror. "She's crying," he stated as if nobody had noticed.

"She's just hungry. I should've fed her before we left, but I thought her daddy might like that job."

The front door clicked shut, and we heard footsteps heading toward us. "Have no fear, Thea, Aunt Sam is here with your beverage of choice."

My heart rate picked up at the sound of her voice, her unique German-American accent. Will's hand tightened around mine, but I couldn't tear my eyes away from the doorway as I waited for Sam to come into sight.

A hand with a bottle appeared first, and my eyes traveled over her, taking in every inch as the rest of her came into view. She was thinner than she'd been when I last saw her, and I had the sudden urge to feed her. Had she not been eating?

"Here, it's still warm," she said as she offered the bottle to Dom, who just stared at it. Sam shook her head. "Just hold it like this, and she'll do the rest," she told him, placing the teat in the baby's mouth. Dom took hold of the bottle, not tearing his eyes away from the baby's face for even a second.

Sam's gaze traveled around the room, stopping on mine and Will's joined hands. I'd expected her to be upset or mad, but a smile played across her lips, and her eyes lifted with it too. She walked over to us, stopping a few feet away, which was too far in my eyes. "Hey!"

Will let go of my hand and closed the distance by pulling her into his arms. "It's good to see you, Samantha." After a second's hesitation, Sam's arms tightened around his back as she returned the hug. They broke apart, and both turned back to me. Sam stepped forward as though she wanted to hug me, but I stood frozen to the spot.

Will waved her toward me. "Don't mind him, it seems he's lost a few brain cells since you walked in the door. Just hug him, and he'll hug you back when he gets control over his body again."

She giggled and took his advice, wrapping her arms around me tentatively. Her caution pulled me out of my stupor, and I was quick to squeeze her back.

"I'm so sorry, Sammy," I whispered against her hair.

She started shaking in my embrace, and I could only assume she was crying since she was holding me so tight with her face pressed against my chest, but I had no way of seeing if I were right. I flicked my worried gaze to Will before checking out the rest of the room. Everyone was occupied with Aimee and the baby, so when I returned my gaze to Will, and he gestured for us to slip out of the room, I lowered my head to whisper in Sam's ear, "Come on, Sammy, we'll find somewhere more private so we can talk."

She discreetly wiped at her eyes as she let me go, and I guided her out of the room behind Will. We had a lot to talk about. Although her actions suggested she wasn't harboring any anger toward me, I needed her to hear my apology. Finally, having her in my arms felt right, and I was well aware she deserved an explanation about how I left Australia before we could even think of moving forward.

I knew for certain both Will and I were on the same page when it came to the future. We wanted Sam in our lives for the long term, and we wanted her to be part of this. *Us.*

The question was, did she want to move forward with us?

EPILOGUE

SAM - TWO YEARS LATER

I ROLLED over in the giant bed I shared with the men in my life and immediately found Matt, who was being the big spoon to my little one. I grinned when I felt another set of hands come to rest against my hip. Matt always slept in the middle, but Will made an effort to ensure he was touching me in some way. It made me feel wanted by both of them because I'd be lying if I didn't admit that when we first started out as a threesome, I was worried since they had all that history, Will was only interested in Matt. Then, I'd fall into the third wheel of the relationship, but he'd made it obvious on more than one occasion in the last two years that he was just as attracted to me as Matt is.

Matt's eyes flickered open, and he pressed a kiss to my forehead. I snuggled in against his chest, inhaling the musk that was pure Matt. I wish I could bottle that scent.

"Morning," Will said, and I could imagine him pressing a kiss to the side of Matt's neck. Will had a thing for necks. He'd run his finger up and down the lengths of either of our necks, the tender action making me weak in the knees pretty much every time.

Matt reached a hand behind him. "Morning, handsome."

"Merry Christmas," I offered, smiling up at Matt and spotting Will glancing over his shoulder.

Matt bent his head to reach my lips, and I opened for him as his tongue probed between the seam. He tightened his hold around me and pulled me over his body until I was sandwiched firmly between the two of them. Will's hand slid over my ass and across my hip, pausing there when I wanted it to travel just a little further. I shifted my ass against his groin, the feel of his hard cock made it more than obvious he was just as aroused as me. I groaned into Matt's mouth.

———

MATT

"Fuck!" I uttered, breaking the kiss and pressing my forehead against Sam's. The noises she made when she was turned-on made my dick hard in seconds every damn time.

She was shifting her body between us, and I lifted her leg, laying it over my hip, opening her up to me. I ran a finger around her clit and over the opening of her pussy. It was warm, wet, and welcoming, and I wanted nothing more than to sink my cock inside, but I needed to make sure she was ready, so I stroked my finger in and out. Will's hand joined mine, and her moans got louder.

"Shit. Kiss her, Matt, or she'll wake the whole house up."

I did as I was told and crushed my lips against hers. Will's commands were always so easy to follow. Ever since the first night the three of us were together, he slipped into the domineering role, and he fucking excelled at it. His commanding tone was sexy, and he always knew exactly what dirty words to say to have both of us like putty in his hands.

We both added another finger each, and Sam moved her hips in a rhythm that demanded us to go faster.

She broke the kiss and sucked in some air. "I need more. I need you both."

I grinned. Those were the words I'd been waiting for. I removed my fingers and lined up my cock, waiting for Will to do the same. He winked at me over her shoulder as I felt him slide his cock against mine and wrap his hand around them both.

"Now! I need you now," Sam demanded as she tried to lower her body to make contact with our dicks.

Will guided our cocks to her entrance, and we all moaned in unison as we inched our way in together. I loved it when Will fucked me and I fucked him, but fuck, this position was my favorite by far. I got to feel them both against me, and I knew I was playing a part to make them both feel good.

We all moved in sync. I watched as Sam turned her head and kissed Will over her shoulder. When they broke the kiss, she leaned forward and took my lips with his as Sam sucked on my neck. I knew I'd have a hickey when she was finished, and I loved that idea so much that my cock twitched. Knowing I wasn't going to last much longer, I slid my hand between Sam and me and rubbed a finger over her clit, needing her to come first.

I circled her clit once, then twice before her pussy clenched around our cocks, and she called out.

"*Yes!*"

The spasms around my cock had my balls tingling, and I soon lost my load inside her against Will's cock with a grunt. "I love you," I said breathlessly to both of them.

I was living a life I never imagined I'd live, and now I couldn't think of a better way to live it, but with these two amazing people, my soul mates, by my side.

———

WILL

Babies' cries crackled through the speakers of the baby monitor on the bedside table, and I groaned. "Not yet." I was so close to coming, but I'd held on wanting the others to reach their climaxes first. I picked up my pace as Sam's pussy still pulsated around us.

Matt pulled out on our joint outward thrust, and I locked my gaze on him, a question I didn't have the words to form on my mind. "I'll deal with that," he offered, nodding to the monitor that was flashing maniacally as the cries were getting more stressed. "You two finish up here."

He pressed a kiss to each of our lips before jumping off the bed and pulling on some boxers. "Have fun," he called over his shoulder as he left the room.

Sam moved, breaking our connection, and I opened my mouth to complain until she turned to face me. "Tell me how you want me, handsome."

"Ride me," I demanded. I loved being in charge in the bedroom, and I knew they both loved that about me too. We really were made for each other.

I rolled onto my back, and Sam made quick work straddling my hips and sinking onto my hard, throbbing cock. We both moaned in pleasure at the sensations it sent through us.

Sam ground her pelvis against mine before lifting herself until she was nearly off my dick and slamming back down again.

"That's it, Samantha, ride me hard."

And she did. She fell into a rhythm that had me panting. I gripped her hips and propelled my own up to meet hers, thrust for thrust. It wasn't long before we were both coming hard. Sam collapsed against my chest, and I wrapped my arms around her, loving the feel of her there.

Just as we were starting to come back to earth, the door opened and closed again, and the sound of babies' grumbling cries entered the room.

"Someone wants cuddles from Mommy and Daddy. Papa cuddles just aren't enough to satisfy these two."

We shifted on the bed so we were both sitting up, the sheet covering us appropriately as Matt made his way toward the bed. "If you two can provide the cuddles, I'll go make their bottles." We each took a baby from him, and after pressing gentle kisses to both babies' foreheads, Matt rushed out of the room once again.

I smiled down at five-month-old Kayden, who resembled his Papa so much with his dark hair and slightly turned-up nose. He gripped my finger with his tiny ones and pulled it toward his mouth. "Hey, little man. Papa's gonna come back with your breakfast in just a minute," I cooed as I pulled my finger out of his reach, and he sucked his fist instead.

"They don't have anything in them anymore," Sam told Jayden, who was trying to find her breast to latch onto but only finding her shoulder. She'd breastfed for the first three months, but it was so draining for her. No sooner had she fed one, and it was time to feed the other. Both Matt and I were so glad when she told us she was going to start them on formula. We were more than ready to help out in the feeding department.

I ran my knuckles over Jayden's fine blond hair and stared down at him in awe. It's been five months since they were born and over a year since we found out it was possible that Sam could've been pregnant to us both at the same time. Heteropaternal superfecundation was what the doctors called it.

We'd discussed getting pregnant for such a long time and

had gone back and forth over how we'd all feel as to who would father the baby. We never imagined that we'd end up fathering a child at the same time. Hell, I didn't even think it was possible, so when the doctors told us the babies were conceived on different days and suggested that because of our unique relationship, there was a chance that a phenomenon could've occurred, I still didn't believe it. It wasn't until the babies were born and the doctors ran their DNA tests that I finally believed it.

We all loved each other so much that it wouldn't have mattered if both babies were mine or Matt's, we'd adore those babies no matter what. We both felt like they were a part of the people we loved, and we'd love them with all our hearts. And that was how we felt now too. We didn't favor one over the other because they were both all of ours.

"Okay. Papa is here with the good stuff." Matt came into the room and handed a bottle to both of us before sitting at the foot of the bed, facing us with his legs crossed. A sad look crossed his face as he watched us feeding our babies, and I knew exactly what had caused that look. We were going to have to leave at the beginning of the new year.

A lot of things had changed in the last two years. We changed record labels due to Gary being a complete moron and trying to pay Aimee off to keep her and Thea away from Dom. We wrote a second country album and were due to go on tour in the spring, our biggest tour yet, which meant as soon as the new year rolled around, we'd be heading back to America to prepare for the tour.

Sam and the twins wouldn't be coming with us initially because we'd be working long days and nights, and Sam would be left on her own with no support. We all decided she'd be better off staying here with Aimee until the tour kicked off. We'd still have a busy schedule, but we'd manage a lot more downtime while traveling between shows. Thankfully, the new record label was so much better than the old one and was happy to work with us in making things easier for our young families.

I placed Kayden over my shoulder and patted his back to get his wind up as I reached out for Matt's hand. He placed it in mine without question. "We're doing the right thing."

Matt nodded. "I know, but that doesn't mean it won't be hard."

Sam cradled Jayden's chin in her hand and leaned his forward as she used the other hand to rub his back in circular motions. "It won't be like the last time we were separated. We'll video call every day… multiple times." Jayden let out a loud belch, and we all laughed.

"As soon as your schedule eases, me, Aimee, and all the kids will be on a flight to wherever you are."

"Speaking of Aimee," I started as I settled a happy Kayden in my arms. "She's gonna be fuming if we don't get to her place on time for Christmas lunch."

Matt reached out for Jayden. "Here, I'll take Jayden while you go get ready."

Sam handed him over without argument and jumped off the bed heading for the bathroom. She glanced at us over her shoulder and stopped at the door. "The four of you are my world. I couldn't imagine living a day without any of you."

"I know the feeling, Sammy. I love you all more than anything," Matt said, his voice breaking with emotion.

I felt the need to lay my heart bare too. "The four of you fill my heart with so much joy. I'm so glad I made my way back to Matt and found you, too. I only existed before, and now I'm living."

Living my best life.

We all were.

If you enjoyed meeting Cole and Scotty, grab their free short story, It's Gotta Be You.

If you like Gay Romance and sexy sports men, check out my novella, Break Away.

If you want to keep up to date with all my book news join my reader group Saffy's Colliding Souls or sign up to my newsletter.

ALSO BY SAFFRON BLU

Running Hearts Series

Running Hurt - *Dom & Aimee*

Running Scared - *Matt, Will & Sam*

Running Wild - *Kat* (Coming 2021)

Running Free - *Al* (Coming 2021)

Standalone

Break Away (M/M)

If you like Paranormal romance, check out my alter ego:

Aimie Jennison

Mount Roxby Series

Pride to Pack

Forever Young and Beautiful

Reclaiming the One

Love of Three (MMF)

Losing Pride

Mount Roxby: Books 1-3 (boxset)

Rossi Pack Series

Releasing the Wolf

Historical Romance

A Knight on the Titanic: A Short Story Inspired by the RMS Titanic

ABOUT THE AUTHOR

Saffron Blu is a romantic at heart. Spending her time writing stories where souls collide, all while looking for her own soul mate.

The mountains and beaches of SE Queensland, Australia, is where Saffron calls home. Her characters are the loudest when she's got her music blaring, drowning out the real world.

For more information:
https://saffronbluauthor.wixsite.com/books
saffronblu.author@gmail.com

Join Saffy's Facebook reader group:
https://www.facebook.com/groups/SaffysCollidingSouls/

facebook.com/SaffronBlu

twitter.com/saffron_blu

instagram.com/saffron_blu

pinterest.com/saffron_blu

amazon.com/author/saffronblu

bookbub.com/authors/saffron-blu

goodreads.com/saffronblu

ACKNOWLEDGMENTS

There are so many people who support me on a daily basis and I love them all dearly for it.

First and foremost, *my family*. Thank you for keeping me grounded and not letting me lose myself in these characters and their worlds.

Kamisa Cole, you girl, go above and beyond to support me. Even when I'm really annoying you—and I know I do that on a daily basis—there you are cheering me on. You'll never know how much you inspire me. This story wouldn't exist if it wasn't for you. Thank you for always believing in me. I love you tons.

Sam Destiny, this one is for you!

Nicki and Kay, thank you for polishing this up to the pretty package it is now. I look forward to working with you on the next one.

Marisa, you really are a cover designing goddess. I love your work.

To anyone reading this, THANK YOU for picking this book up and giving it a chance. YOU are incredible!